I HEARD A FISH CRY
and other stories

I HEARD A FISH CRY
and other stories

A Collection Of Short Stories By

CAROLYN LIGHT BELL

Adelaide Books
New York / Lisbon

2018

I Heard a Fish Cry
and Other Stories
a collection of short stories
by Carolyn Light Bell

Published by Adelaide Books, New York / Lisbon
An imprint of the Istina Group DBA
adelaidebooks.org

Editor-in-Chief
Stevan V. Nikolic

For any information, please address Adelaide Books
at info@adelaidebooks.org

ISBN13: 978-0-9996451-0-9
ISBN10: 0-9996451-0-2

Printed in the United States of America

For Eddie, with love

Preface

In this collection of lovingly-crafted stories, *I Heard a Fish Cry*, Carolyn Light Bell portrays animals as witness, alter ego, adversary, and foil to illuminate human fallibility. These satirical, often playful, stories leave us questioning our own intelligence.

Light Bell is far-reaching in her scope and is unafraid to take on the subtleties of class, animal rights, generational differences and sex. People in these stories advocate, fear, exploit, or defend a variety of creatures, including wolves, cats, dogs, birds, cougars, and bulls, dead or alive. Animals, in turn, reveal particular qualities in human behavior that leave us vulnerable. As the stories evolve, the reader discovers that within the heart and soul of every human being lies a deep, biological connection to all animals.

The title story features an animal rights activist whose mission to protect an endangered environment counterbalances her mission to find a mate. "On the Peak to Peak Express," "Wolf Cubs and Convicts," and "Forced Entry" explore the limits of human freedom. "Katy's Farm" and "Pulling Calves" shock the reader with their blunt depiction of nature's harsh justice. "Childhood Games" and "A Lamb Bash" explore issues of class, religion, and power. "Why I

Fight with Bobbie but Not Billie" depicts characters grappling with theories of science versus real observation. "Condor's Raw Side" is a poignant, comical story of loyalty. In "Harold in His Boxer Shorts," a half-naked man is locked out of his home by his dog. "Catch and Kill" explores the belief in fishing as innocent sport. "Skateboards and a Sheepdog" peels off a layer or two of fear that comes with age. "Cow and Bull Stories" describe the tender vulnerability of three generations as they struggle with individual challenges—all set against the backdrop of a drowning cow seeking refuge in a canoe and a horny bull on a rampage.

Acknowledgements

These short stories have originally appeared in the following printed magazines and publications online:

"Anthony Birde" first appeared in *Paterson Literary Review*

"I Heard A Fish Cry," "Childhood Games," and "Catch and Kill" first appeared in *Praxis, Gender and Cultural Critiques,* 2006

"On the Peak to Peak Express" first appeared in *Forge,* 2012

"Canaries and Krumkakes" first appeared in *Dos Passos Review,* 2013

"The Lamb Bash" first appeared in *Griffin,* 2012

"Why I Fight With Bobbie and Not Billie" first appeared in *Big Muddy,* 2008

"Harold in His Boxer Shorts" first appeared in *Limestone,* 2008

"Condor's Raw Side" first appeared in *Great Midwestern Quarterly,* 1998

"Pulling Calves" first appeared in *Northern Plains Quarterly*

"Hansel and Gretel" first appeared in *Stickman Review*, 2014

"Katy's Farm" first appeared in *Westwind Review*, 2007

"Cow and Bull Stories" first appeared in *Louisiana Literature*, 2009

"Forced Entry" first appeared in *Tales of the Unanticipated*, 1996

"All He Saw was Summer" first appeared in *Amarillo Bay*, 2011

"Stories from Old Pines" first appeared in *Cottonwood*, 2014

"Skateboards and a Sheepdog" first appeared in *Adelaide Literary Magazine*, 2017

Contents

I Heard a Fish Cry

I kept on dragging myself to these parties, up out of my agoraphobic angst, because I refused to believe it was hopeless. Hope was all there was, for God's sake, *the thing with feathers that perches in the soul.* Yet, it took me hours to cover up deepening facial lines reflecting anxiety about the broken world, an off-the-charts libido, and a stay-at-home-under-the-covers need to be alone. At 33, I finally understood what Demeter, my surrogate mother, meant when she said, "We feminists have lost a hell of a lot of ground. We're falling into a fucking abyss." Most guys were too self-absorbed to notice. I wasn't blond, petite, or submissive.

Each attempt was a performance piece. I soaked cotton balls with witch hazel, closed my eyes, thinking *tranquility,* opened them, hoping for renewed sparkle, applied mascara and kohl for dramatic effect, popped in contacts, and said to myself, "Arise, slumbering fools. Look deep into the windows of my soul. I am so worth it!" I put on a moderately daring décolletage and carefully arranged my breasts to suggest cleavage. Lastly, I layered three lipstick tones, all red.

On the Myers-Briggs test, a hokey but convenient personality inventory based on Jungian principles, I learned

I was an ENTJ, which meant that I was an Extroverted-Intuitive-Thinking-Judging person. Myers-Briggs was one of a battery of self-tests I took as a stopgap measure to make sure there was nothing seriously wrong with me. Demeter tried to pretend she wasn't worried, and suggested therapy as a means to an end. I agreed on the end, but not on the means, never on the means. I had zero tolerance for waiting in an office decorated in computer-generated prints of sunsets, stained in passive shades of lavender, where a shrink welcomed me in a whispering voice, dirty beard, wrinkled shirt, and sandals barely covering his white feet and torn yellow toenails.

Lunch with a brutally honest friend was less agonizing.

Comparing myself to others on large-scale graphs was often confusing, filling me with self-doubt, even though other females I knew in their late thirties were at least as desperate as I was, especially the ISFP or Introverted-Sensing-Feeling-Perceiving types. My introverted friends had a terrible time, always stewing, always anxious, androphobic, mysophobic, xenophobic. One friend was afraid of an erect penis: medorthophobic.

On the MMPI, I was high on the OCD scale, but grateful I filled no other categories on the DSM-IV List of Mental Disorders. It was the rest of the world that was screwed up. At least I hadn't gone online to get laid. Match-dot-com. Harmony-dot-com. Not for me. Hump-dot-com. I needed to meet people in the flesh, bump up against them. Feel their chemistry. Smell their pheromones.

The room was packed. Although I liked people, I also had an ear condition called BPPV or Benign Positional

Paroxysmal Vertigo, which meant that in a noisy crowd, I had little staying power, feeling dizzy and disoriented. If new people weren't immediately captivating, my head spun, my body started to twitch, and I felt an urgent need to run away.

Over in the corner, the guy sitting in an amber corduroy armchair was kind of cute, but his hair and teeth were a little too straight, a sign of inflexible sexism. Nevertheless, I was drawn to his posture, the way he inhabited the area, an "I own my space" kind of certainty. He was helping himself to generous handfuls of M&M's out of a glass bowl. I liked M&M's, but I didn't like the new colors. Intense blue chocolate put me off. I'd been eating red for so many years, it was hard to adjust. I also suspected they'd gotten a few millimeters smaller.

M&M's knees were spread wide and he was talking with another guy in a moderate but self-assured voice about various gauges of hunting rifles and dogs. The other guy, whose hair hung limply in a long, straggly ponytail, was stretched out sloppily on the sofa next to M&M. He was wearing stained jeans and an orange T-shirt that had some kind of chainsaw logo on it. Being in the very presence of someone like Ponytail made me want to dig in my bag for hand sanitizer. I hung around, waiting for an opportunity to interrupt M&M. Since I knew little about guns, ten minutes passed before I felt it was time to interject. Finally, the men shifted the subject back to dogs and seemed to settle there, where I found myself in familiar territory.

"Your standard setter, now there's a dog," Ponytail said. "Jumpy, but fast as hell goin' after quarry."

"You mean Irish setter or something else?" M&M had deep-set sapphire eyes, not exactly my type, but passable. He sat up straighter, moved in head to head with Ponytail.

"Naw, English, ya know, the spotted ones. Brits are like, ya know, like, more tight-ass than the Irish. You could call 'em more refined. Easier to handle." Ponytail cranked his head around to look at me standing over them. "I whistle. She comes, if ya know what I mean. Name's Betsy. Like for the Queen. Get it? Elizabeth? Betsy?" He threw his head back and laughed. I could see his rear molars, an area I didn't particularly want to see because there was residue of ground-up food particles deep within. I preferred smart-eyed, articulate types.

I made a quick decision. M&M liked Irish setters, which were playful by nature. I plunked myself down next to him and broke right into the conversation. "Every setter I ever knew was wild. How do you train a dog like that?"

The men said nothing, as if they hadn't heard or didn't know I was there. "Slide over," I said, wiggling into the couch, and then, facing each one of them squarely, "Soooo, you guys like to hunt and fish?"

"Yeah. Hunting's cool. Maybe kind of a guy thing, though, I guess." M&M looked at Ponytail and then back at me and smiled, licking the chocolate off his palm.

Ponytail said, "Bet you're one of those Bambi lovers. Well, hate to break it to ya, little girl, animals don't have feelings."

M&M adjusted his buttocks in the chair, adjusting both flanks down into the cushion as far as he could, settling in. He straightened his back to look up at me, checking me out. "Don't mind Neil here. He can be a little brutal. He doesn't mean anything by it. Just a dumb ass." He licked his fingers, one at a time, slurping noisily. I decided not to move even though his manners were unappetizing. "My name's James." He stuck out his dry hand.

"Which animal can't feel?" I didn't extend my hand. My volume was on Medium High. It had taken some doing to catch their attention. I wasn't ready to release. M&M was still a weak possibility. I recrossed my legs. "Fish can't feel. Have you ever heard a fish say ouch? Sorry, didn't catch your name." He leaned forward to look at me, curving up one side of his mouth into a smirk. Ponytail snickered.

"Actually, yes, once I actually heard a fish cry," I said.

"Cry?" Ponytail raised an eyebrow.

"Yes. Know what a yellowfin is? They put little pieces of it on sushi." I didn't wait for him to respond. "Well, I was in a small boat south of Tulum with a tiny Mayan guy who motored around for about an hour until he found a spot where he thought yellowfins were biting. Before I could bait and throw in my line, the guy tore a live crab apart claw by claw, threw each segment into the ocean to attract other fish, and reeled one into the boat. Its fins were yellow... like daffodils! Parts of its body were blue as a glacier. Absolutely incredibly beautiful." I watched M&M's face for signs of emotion. Not finding any, I raised my volume to High. "And it screamed!" I said. Then I dipped my voice to Low for dramatic flair. "The yellowfin screamed in grief." I flattened my lips and sharpened my teeth on the two "f's," simulating fish torture. My head spun. The BPPV was kicking in.

"Right. And I'm God," Ponytail said, laughing. He rose up out of the sofa. "I'll let you two figure this one out. I need another beer," he said, disappearing into the crowd.

"It really happened. It had a hoarse scream." I stuck out my hand. "My name's Eurydice."

"Wow. How Greeky! You'll have to forgive me. I've never heard a fish cry. And I've never heard a horse scream either. Sorry, Eurydice."

"Not horse as in neigh, neigh. Hoarse. H-O-A-R-S-E. I never want to hear it again. It said, 'I have children at home. I have a family. I have coral to see and waters to swim and you're taking them all from me. This hook really hurts. Take it out.'" I knew I was tipping the OCD scale now. But someone had to fight for the rights of fish. Someone had to educate the poor, dumb slobs of the world. It didn't matter if M&M didn't buy it right off. Skepticism was healthy. He'd think about it later. It was my responsibility as a TJ person to help him understand. I paused. Hearing no response, I continued.

"My name means justice, wide justice. When I was in the sixth grade, I read in my Weekly Reader that giraffes have no voice. I was stupid enough to believe it until I went to Africa. Then I heard a giraffe grunt. After that, I stopped believing in other people's animal facts. I believe what I can see and hear."

"How do you know it wasn't the driver, grunting I mean?" said M&M, rocking his weight forward, looking for just the right moment to escape.

"Just f—off, would'ja?" I shouted, surprising myself.

Another man stepped forward and sat on the arm of the sofa. He'd been on the periphery of the circle of chairs, but now he looked directly at me, peering over the rims of his trifocals. M&M slouched back. It was one thing to choose to lose, but quite another to be one-upped by some preppy jerk. This guy was dressed in a black turtleneck sweater tucked into dark slacks, nattily trimmed with a black braided belt. He had thick, wavy hair, graying at the temples.

I blinked back at him. His eyes were warm as fur. I stood up, squared my feet, and faced him.

"How would you describe the voices of whales?" he asked in a low voice, leaning toward me.

My head suddenly cleared. Someone understood my truth. I was an expert in fish voices. I answered with great authority. "Whales sing. Through their mouths. With sonar." I swallowed and continued, "They sing just for the hell of it. Have you ever heard humpbacks sing?"

"Yes. Mystical. Very mystical. It puts me in touch with my liquidity. What's beyond the bumper-to-bumper. I pop in my humpback CD and I'm there. In the sea."

"Wow. That's great. Whales instead of road rage. Did you know they call that Intermittent Explosive Disorder? Which one do you have?"

"I don't have intermittent anything."

"No, I mean which humpback CD?"

"Oh, I don't know. I found it at Cheapo Discs when I was looking for Thelonious Monk."

"Which Monk?"

"You don't do jazz?"

"Yes. I 'do' jazz." I hated that expression. "Doing" music sounded supercilious, bordering on trifling. "But Cheapo has its music in categories, like Rock and Roll,

Western, R and B, Female Vocalists, Country, Jazz. How come the whale CD was next to jazz?"

"Call it intuition."

"I don't get it." He was a bit strange, but I liked that.

"Some genius salesclerk filed it there, sensing a guy like me would come along. She knew we don't have to stay in any one assigned category. We can mix it up. Just because your name is Eurydice doesn't mean you can't move off the earth. And just because my name is Nereus doesn't mean I'm stuck in water. We can survive in other elements." He looked up at me slyly.

I thought he was an interesting blend of my Myers-Briggs complement, and something else I couldn't name. I also thought he was peering down my dress to find what he couldn't see. I'd made the wrong wardrobe choice. I felt objectified when men pretended to care about my ideas just so they could take me to bed. It was always a toss-up between putting a sack over my head and strutting my stuff.

I threw him a heavier line. "Talk about survival, did you know we're overfishing the ocean? Doesn't that make you feel guilty? I mean I hardly want to order tuna anymore. So many species are already extinct."

"I find guilt a complete waste of time. Caviar tastes excellent with champagne."

M&M got up with visible effort, farted softly, and walked away.

"Well, I like fish too, but we're absolutely raping the environment." I couldn't break free of my need to press home the point. "Snowmobilers chase deer out of the woods. Polar bears are drowning from melting ice. The cassowaries in Australia are pissed off because their gum trees are going."

"Cass-o-whaties?"

"Cassowaries, the only frugivore large enough to disperse plant species in Queensland's rain forests. They're attacking Australians with their spurs."

"I like it when you say the 'fru' part. Your mouth makes a rose… I don't suppose you want to explain frugivores?"

"It's an animal that prefers fruit. So, anyway, my point is we're polluting the land and the ocean too. It's nothing more than a slop bucket for cruise liners." I was talking too fast. I didn't often get a captive audience. I could hardly keep up with myself.

"Exactly what does an ocean liner throw into the ocean? I mean I thought they'd stopped that."

"Fluorescent lightbulbs, waste, uneaten food, plastics. They all get dumped."

"Where do you get your information? Could you say 'frugivore' again?"

"I trip over the stuff when I'm shelling all over. Mexico, Malaysia, Africa, you name it. Instead of marginellas and wentletraps, what do I find? Plastic shoes, doll arms, long glass tubes, and garbage bags."

"Hmmm, marginellas and wentletraps. How do you know ocean liners are the culprits? Maybe it's the beachfront resorts."

"I saw pictures in the National Geographic of the contents of an albatross chick's stomach. Its mother had fed it cigarette lighters, broken clothespins, a pump-top sprayer, a peanut shell, and so much garbage that there was no room for real fish food. Poor little chick starved to death."

"No decent, self-respecting albatross mother would feed it those things."

"Do you have any children?" I felt bold. He seemed concerned about the mother-infant nurturing bond.

"Not yet," he said, "but I'd like a whole mess of them. The non-frugivore type. The type that sing just for the hell of it, into the wind and waves. And I'd teach them to have no guilt."

"It's so sick what we've done to the ocean. A mother albatross feeds her chick what she finds in the gyres." What was I thinking? It was way premature to talk about kids. And I was letting him talk me into things like no guilt. How could I restore justice to a world without guilt? Didn't that mean no conscience?

"What's a gyre?" He took my hand and held it firmly.

"It's like a crevasse in a current. A sort of black hole. The mom can't really see what's in there. She just plucks out a bunch of stuff she thinks is food for her baby."

My head felt light, giddy.

"You're really over the top, did you know that?" He removed his glasses, folding the bows over the neck of his sweater, and smiled. He had a narrow space between his front teeth, a sure sign of vulnerability. Vulnerability was vital.

"What top?"

"Never mind. I like it." He stepped closer to my side, pressed his nose down into my hair, inhaled, and faced me, wrapping both arms around my waist.

"People think human beings are the best species to walk the planet, but we're systematically destroying the homes of most other creatures. It's a holocaust of animals." I could smell his salty breath.

He kept one arm around my waist and, with his other hand, reached across for my hand and placed it on his chest so I could feel his heart beating. He threaded his fingers through mine. Any moment I might faint, but I didn't pull away.

"And then there's the oil well noise. Offshore drillers pump oil—thump, thump, like a giant heartbeat out of the ocean—and can be heard a hundred miles away underwater. How would you like to hear that thumping all day long? Pretty soon there won't be any whales to sing." I needed to hear my voice.

"That'll be the end of Judy Collins and the humpbacks. We'll have to do all the humping, I mean sonar." He smiled.

I suspected he might be humoring me. "So that's the one you listen to? I have it too." His eyes were dark as the ocean floor, where strange creatures lurked. I was swimming in his essence, airless, flapping slowly. I restrained myself from licking the algae I imagined to be floating over his eyelids. Kelp was good for the nervous system.

"And the end of music for meditation and yoga and Shiatsu."

"You do yoga too?" I was hyperventilating.

"You look flexible. Are you?" He unfolded his glasses and put them back on, raising his head up and down to examine me from head to toe.

"If whales can't sing, they get depressed and die." I imagined his body was sleek when it was wet.

"I like Bikram where I can get hot." He pressed his lips against my hands.

"Yuk. I hate it when people's sweat flies onto the mirror. It splashes all over and onto my face. Big waves of sweat. I like Iyengar better. I don't feel like throwing up."

"Maybe there oughta be whale shrinks," he said.

I could put justice aside just this once. I was tired, so tired of waiting. I didn't care about whales as much as I cared about his eyes and how I would melt into them when he rose up over me, his back a great hump, flukes slapping the sheets, and me, riding the waves, sending loud cries into the air to be carried hundreds of miles away, jettisoning the waste of my hopeful life into the great sea.

On the Peak to Peak Express

There we were, on the Peak to Peak Express, sniffing the air, inhaling the grandeur of the rugged dramatic Blackcomb and Whistler mountains in British Columbia, innocently discussing a friend's divorce, when a starkly handsome young man caught my eyes and held them.

"Would you do me a *favor?*" he asked in an Australian accent, favor sounding more like *fiva*.

"Sure, what?"

"Would you take my picture here?" Definitely an Aussie. Take came out as tyke between his perfect teeth.

"I'd be happy to."

My skiing companion and I traded looks.

"But first," he added, "I have to get something out of my pocket and put it on."

I knew something strange was about to take place and began to feel wary.

A sign above his head read: **This is the longest and highest single gondola ride in the world.**

Anything might happen. There was time.

I established my boundaries immediately. "You're not going to strip, are you?"

"Oh no," he said, reaching deep into the nether regions of his belongings. I'm not sure from where exactly, he pulled

out and unfolded an enormous rubber horse's head. It was a very large, grotesque head, with wide flaring nostrils, mouth agape, and huge teeth set in a decidedly hungry expression.

The man handed me his camera.

"Show me where to push it," I said.

The man, in a colorful confetti-decorated snow jacket, closed my hand over the proper button and posed in various postures, cheesecake-like, crumpling his silky jacket under him. Whistler Peak with its single Black Tusk loomed up behind him. I snapped several shots, centering them as close to the middle of his huge long nose as possible in the little green square on his tiny digital screen. Perspective was distorted since his horse head was enormous and our space confined. His beastly mane was framed by vast, snow-covered slopes.

My friend, a horse woman, whinnied.

He was encouraged. He cocked his horsey head at her, removed his rubber mask and grinned with the surprise of joy. Maskless, his face had the sculpted bones of a Grecian and the ruddy cheeks of an Italian.

I handed the camera back to him. "I hope those will work for you," I said.

My friend was still whinnying impatiently, probably waiting to get out of the barn. He handed her the horse head. She struggled to put it on.

"Now I'll take your picture," he said. Dressed entirely in black, she donned her black gloves for hooves, reared up on her hind legs, and pawed the air, snorting loudly. I was dwarfed beneath her stallion-like wildness. Terrified, thrilled, and amused, I whinnied too.

She sat down, removed the mask, and returned it to him. He was impressed. She had outdone him.

He put the horse head on again. "May I ask you to do me one more favor? This is where it gets a bit pornographic."

"You're not going to strip, are you?" This time it was a dare.

"No, no."

"Well, all right then."

He stretched out on the bench, heavy ski boots clunking down on the metal seat, assuming a seductive pose. His outer arm lay at rest along his ski-panted leg. His other arm was bent under his head, to keep it from lolling about in the pitch and sway of the gondola.

He lay there without moving. Benign. Maybe even smug. I pushed the little silver button. Snowy mountains behind him remained stately, remote, and quiet. The tram rocked. His horsiness sat up, took off his mask, and spoke. "I've had my picture taken all over with this horse head on."

He handed me his camera proudly, displaying shots from Cairo to Madrid.

The photographs were dark and opaque in the glare of winter sun shining through the tram windows. "Interesting," I said. "Why?"

"I'm in the horse business. I buy and sell Arabians." He lowered his gallant head and tucked his folded mask back somewhere deep within the folds of his heavy clothing.

"Oh," I said. I wanted to ask, "What are you doing later?"

The gondola reached its mid-peak destination. We all stood up, skis, poles, and boards in hand, returning to our less equine roles.

Somewhere in the whistle of wind, high in the Douglas firs, I'll be listening for his whinnying as he thunders down the slopes.

Anthony Birde

I made up my last name like I make up my life. On the spot. I can cruise right over things if I want. So it's Birde with an e for elusion. Having a fake name's good when schools ask questions. Like where I'm from and who my mama is. They don't gotta know.

I've been in so many of these so-called Institutions of Learning, I lost count. I don't know how long before I terminate my residency in this one too. Most teachers suck and the dudes is no better. They look right past me steada at me. Like yesterday, in Science. Woke up in the middle of a lecture that was stuck on the same note as when I put my head down on my desk. No change. Somethin' about cells. All outa a musty ratty ole' book. I swear I coulda slept a lifetime and I wouldna missed a beat. Makes you wonder. What does all this school shit got to do with my life?

I mean last night someone found this big football dude shot and dropped in the alley. Two days they said he was lyin' there. Just last week he scored the winning touchdown. Now he's food for the rats. So I took this big ole' honkin' safety pin off the shoulder of my jacket where I'd been savin' it and jammed it right into my lip. The lower one. Burned like hell but I knew I was alive when the chick next to me

looked at it, got all squirmy and moved to a different seat. Bell rang so I decided to chill in English.

We read some cool stuff in that class. At least she doesn't yammer at us all period. So when I walked in and took up the desk by the door, I didn't think she'd notice. But, she sees shit right off. I could tell by the look on her face she was gettin' wound up for some kinda blastoff. She looked like she was gonna pass out—all pale-faced and big-eyed. I smiled at her thinking that'd make her feel better.

"What...did you do, Anthony?"

Wasn't it obvious? The woman blind? But I copped to it. "Did it fifth hour." My lip was starting to swell up like a balloon.

"The mouth is full of germs," she said. "It's like the nose. It collects bacteria."

"Just came from biology. Don't need another germ lecture."

"You could get a terrible infection."

"If it gets infected, I'll take it out. Piercing's cool. Dudes do it to all parts of their bodies. Look at you. Your ears is pierced. You got holes runnin' all up and down your ears like a goddamned woodpecker been atcha."

She put her hands up to her ears. "But there's a difference between nose and ear cartilage and the tissue in your mouth and lips. Don't do it. Take it out!" She kinda plucked at my jacket. I just kept grinning at her, all full of myself. Usually that works. Mama used to say I'm a pretty cool lookin' dude. I got skin the color of caramel apples you get around here in the fall and my eyes are kinda big and droopy-like. Gets me places.

I could tell she wanted to mother me. My real Mom is supposed to send me a plane ticket to go back to L.A. but she's got somethin' else fryin' in her pan. There've been no letters for me. "Don't hold your breath," my ole' man said. "You can stay here, but don't cramp my style and stay outta jail."

I don't mind livin' on Nicollet Island with him. It's the stinkin' goats and chickens runnin' around in people's yards. I grew up on concrete in the City of Angels. But, I'm not rushin' to get back there either. Hell, people on my tail. No matter where I go. Like Batwoman. That woman is evil. She won't quit til she like gets me in her cave, I swear. She lives across the street and there's no way to hop a bus for school except to pass her yard. She's like waitin' on me. Chick's got a weird way of sayin' hello. She clings to that front door, open just for the occasion, pretends she's sweepin' or somethin'. Then she lowers this black lace nightgown off one shoulder. She kinda tosses her head back to invite me in and licks her lips till they're all wet as pussy. Sometimes she calls out, "Hey, baby!" The way I look at it, birds and bats don't mix. I fly, man, I fly.

"Someone might tear it out of your mouth."

She was still standing in front of my desk. I could feel my cheeks squinch up again. It's this habit I have. Squinch, squinch, squinch, three times my cheeks go off. It's called a tic. Keeps me from hauling off and derailin' dudes who get too close. I only did that once and next thing I knew I was in the slammer with a record and a parole officer. Left all that behind in L.A. Cops is cops. Sometimes they're suits who say they're out to help me and then boom! They're harrassin' the hell out of me.

"I won't let 'em," I told her.

It was Wednesday—time to group up and talk about a story we'd been reading. Bout this Puerto Rican dude. Bout a flag. It was a cool story. I had plenty to say about it, but soon as I pulled up my desk, everyone moved away.

They don't know how hard it is to get a bath where I live. Water is barely an inch wide and it ain't hot. There's no place to sleep 'cept on the floor on a bunch of dirty ole' rags he keeps in the corner for cleaning up. He ain't exactly accommodatin'. In L.A. I had a couple of changes. Here I got but one set of clothes—t-shirt, sweatshirt, jeans and my rad boots. All black. I'm a black bird.

I shave my head to keep the lice out. Except for one strip right down the middle. I bleach it out. It's like really cool. I run a heavy chain around my boots and on my jacket. Leather's hip, man. Besides, Minnesota gets some nasty weather.

The safety pin was one I took off this baby stroller. The kid's mama'd left the kid outside the 7-11. That kills me. Anybody could hijack the little dude or use him for bait. Or he could get caught in crossfire. Seen it happen. If I ever have a kid, I'm gonna watch him better'n that. These are some dangerous times. The pin was all shiny and held a blue rattle right above the kid's eyes. Kid looked like he wanted it, so I unstuck the pin and put the rattle in the kid's fist. Kid didn't even bawl. Looks hip on my lip. Think I'll pierce my navel next. No one'll see it 'cept who I decide. And she'll have to live on the fly.

Canaries and Krumkakes

I love alleys. Tall, bright pink hollyhocks, brilliant yellow day lilies, and variegated hosta bloom along a few edges. Others sport heaps of abandoned equipment no longer of interest such as tricycles, ten-foot basketball hoops, and other things that rust away forgotten since they're outsized for garbage trucks.

So much is revealed behind houses, in the butt ends of lives. Some folks choose to line up their trash cans in even rows, carefully placing their tied-up garbage in neat, white plastic bags with red ribbons, like fresh laundry. Other folks tip their kitchen and bathroom wastebaskets upside down and just pour everything in—coffee grounds, used tissues, plastic clamshells, chicken bones—all sticky, odorous offerings to the garbage gods.

As for recycling, the world's last-ditch effort to save the planet from burial by trash, you can see how we live based on our recycling bins. When old-style bins' flimsy lids hang off the hinges, one finds all manner of recyclables: empty bottles of beer tossed from dark, empty living rooms where obese Americans lie on their couches bleary-eyed; paper sacks stuffed with crunched-up Mountain Dew cans and folded-up pizza boxes from fast-food devotées; tidily bundled New York Times and bottles of Prosecco from bright, warm, forty-year-olds' granite-countered kitchens; cheery Starbucks cups with little cardboard holders, from bins of thirty-something fanatic athletics who just finished their nonfat muffins after sprinting a ten-mile run.

It's all exposed in the alley.

You may wonder how I know so much about garbage. No, I am not a dumpster diver, although I admit to occasionally opening a can or two for the distinct purpose of depositing my double-bagged dog poops when I'm far from home and don't wish to carry the bags great distances. I tuck my used bags inside garbage bags already deposited in the trash cans. If the garbage cans are empty, I seek out a full one. Hence, I have seen a lot of garbage styles.

I have driven down our fair city's streets on a windy day and seen huge, empty, plastic milk jugs chasing entire Sunday newspapers, all whirling toward the lake, away from households who don't secure their recycling bins.

New Year's Day was a rich day for exploring. I was rambling alleyways through deep snow, reviewing the overflowing garbage of our former neighborhood with my two favorite Bearded Collie sheepdogs, Shadrach and Mishach, who were, in turn, padding over crusty ice to find the best pooping spot. Marshall, my husband, was home sleeping. Shadrach is fourteen and has IBS (irritable bowel syndrome), so it's either fake-squat as in constipation or squat-in-a-hurry as in diarrhea. In either case, it's better done in the back alley rather than on the front boulevard.

Heading down our old stomping grounds held purpose for me. I'd received an inviting voice mail. While we were out of town, our former neighbors, Hans and Mary Andersson, had called to tell us that their annual gift of krumkakes were baked and ready. A krumkake is a thin, crisp, rolled crepe meant to be eaten over a plate in one or two quick bites because it crumbles all over your clothes as soon as it's pierced by teeth. The taste is glorious, but protective aprons or washable duds are a must.

A pumpkin-colored glow emanated from the Anderssons' kitchen window—surely a sign Hans was awake making something delicious in the kitchen. Of Norwegian descent, his krumkakes are tantalizing—flaky and delicate, with a hint of vanilla or almond, subtly aromatic, reminiscent of plump, rosy-cheeked, aproned women, fjords, and frigid water. Hans is tall and lanky with a shock of thick white hair. I opened the gate, the dogs bounded ahead, and I plunged heavily through knee-high drifts to rap a mittened greeting on the big picture window. Hans' smiling face appeared through the glass. He and I share a love for early morning visits. He opened the back door wide, and I tried to avert my eyes from the gaping front of his pajama bottoms.

Did I mention it was 7 a.m.?

"Morning, Hans!" I shouted, happy he was up, but reluctant to close the distance between us. "We came for our krumkakes!"

"We-e-l-l-ll, look who's here!" he bellowed. "You look radiant! Beautiful!"

"Marshall and I just got back from Montreal, where we skied through mountain fairylands!" I said.

"And we're getting ready to drive to Rushford to pick up a canary," he said, "so I can't invite you in."

"Oh, that's okay. We got your message and stopped by to see if your offer of krumkakes was still open. Are they all gone? What kind of canary?"

"A red one," he said, smiling broadly, showing the gap between his front teeth.

Mary appeared at the door. "Hello!" she said, smiling beneficently.

"Happy New Year to you!" I said to Mary.

Hans disappeared while Mary and I exchanged pleasantries. When he returned, he held an enormous cage high above his head. An elaborate wooden birdcage with narrow slats and three doors. His expression was nothing if not grand.

"That's for the canary?" I said. "It's big enough for a whole family of canaries. Why don't you breed them? Breeding's fun!" I offered, considering myself an expert in the art of breeding animals since I loved the hell out of breeding Beardies.

"We can get only one male because they won't sing if there are two."

"And a female?" I asked.

"They don't sing," he said and began a pretty long-winded story considering the fact that he was still in his pajamas.

"We once had a canary named Essence, but we left the front door open one afternoon, and the Bergs' cat sneaked in, tipped over the cage, and killed Essence."

"What? The Bergs' cat? You've got to be kidding!" I gasped in disbelief. "Hysterical!" I broke into spasms of laughter right there, dropping to my knees in the snowbank.

My reaction wasn't meant to be cruel. I wasn't happy the canary had been murdered. Believe me. Hans and I both knew that.

"Whenever did that happen? Recently?"

"No," Mary said, "it was a long time ago, when Hansie Junior was a kid. Hans called me up from downtown all excited to surprise me. 'The three of us will be ready at five thirty,' he said. 'Pick us up at the delivery door.' I can still see Hansie Junior coming out of the department store, clutching a small brown paper sack, so carefully, like it was glass. He showed me what was inside—a tiny little canary."

"So, if Hansie is thirty-five now, you lost Essence, your first bird, more than twenty-five years ago."

Mary looked solemnly at me and raised her whitening eyebrows. "You know what it's like when one of your favorite things is gone? You can't ever replace it. Mrs. Berg offered to buy us a new one, but I just couldn't do it. For months afterwards, I would find little bits of birdseed, red and yellow and brown, in little cracks in the kitchen floor tile, and I would pick them up and roll them over and over in my hands and think about Essence…and I just cried and cried."

★

For nineteen years Marshall and I and our children lived on the same block with the Anderssons and Bergs. I'm not sure if it was our children, our dogs, or us that the Bergs hated most. The Bergs were impotent to punish us personally from much of anything, so they picked on our offspring and our pets. They didn't allow our children to play in their front yard with their children and told them so. They hated our dogs pooping on their boulevard, even though we were always attached on the other end with a leash and a plastic bag ready for immediate poop retrieval.

I couldn't stop the desecration of the Bergs' boulevard as a grassy site of choice of our beautiful dogs with their genetic tendency toward unpredictable bowels. Samoset, our first Beardie and a very independent guy, deposited his breakfast and dinner squarely on their lovely green boulevard. Every ensuing Beardie we had, including whole litters of puppies, would prance down the street, eschewing every other spot, only to sniff out the Bergs' lovely patch of carefully tended grass. I stuffed my pockets with ample numbers of plastic bags to pick up their droppings. However, in their waning years, our dogs' intestinal products became looser and looser until it was no longer easy to remove all trace of their offerings.

Whenever he spotted us, Ned Berg sprang from his house to holler, "Get your dog off my lawn!" Often my dog would be in full rounded squat at the very instant Ned emerged. Samoset's timing incensed Ned and kept me hypervigilant. Naturally, I had nothing to say after Samoset had already spread out his garden of delights. I would only smile weakly and remove as much of it as I could. Ned had no sympathy for elderly dogs and didn't appreciate my explanation of Samoset's health issues.

Our outraged children reported that they regularly saw Ned walking his golden retriever into the nursing home side yard down the street, looking away when the dog dumped his load, not picking it up. "Why doesn't Mr. Berg have to pick up after his own dog?" our children asked. We had no answer.

If it came to a civil suit, I would plead that the boulevard did not technically belong to the Bergs. It belonged to the city. Therefore, Samoset was legally entitled to squat on anybody's boulevard. That gave me a great deal of inner satisfaction but didn't keep me from being on guard.

Try as I might, I couldn't please the Bergs. They preferred warfare. Once Ned threw a heavy ring of keys at our dogs. I can still hear Samoset's yelp of surprise. When our children grew from infancy to early adulthood, we moved six blocks away. It was difficult to avoid the Bergs completely since their house was on the way to the dog-walking area, the grocery store, and the beach—everywhere I wanted to go.

There was one odd thing, though, that made me feel queasy inside. After nineteen antagonistic years, Ned Berg sent me a photograph he'd taken of me many years ago, crossing the street, pushing a stroller with our barefoot middle child. It was a flattering portrait, featuring me as a young mother in shorts and a brief knit top, sporting the long, flowing hair and sandals of the seventies. The photograph looked like a National Enquirer candid because I was caught mid-action, licking my lips, hair in my face, focused on pushing the stroller. I don't remember his taking the picture and felt a slight chill creep up my spine when I opened up the envelope. A second odd thing is that when we were building our new house, I regularly spotted Ned's wide rear end in quick retreat down the street after he'd been ogling the construction site. Just out walking or stalking? I wasn't sure.

"Tell you what," Hans broke into my reverie. "I'll come by your house in an hour and drop off the krumkakes."

"Fine, Hans. Great! Glad I stopped! Can't wait! Thank you!"

I walked home with Shadrach and Mishach, musing to myself about the canary killing. The Bergs' cat snuffed out Hans' Essence! Ned Berg's cat committed a Break and Enter and subsequent Canaracide. My dogs' behavior couldn't compare. What a great way to start the new year! Ned's self-righteousness flown back on its feathers!

Hans came to our door a few hours later, krumkakes in hand, wearing a sheepish grin. I gave him a big kiss on the cheek. My husband woke up, and between us, we relished every last krumkake, ignoring flaky crumbs all over our clothes, musing over the demise of the Anderssons' original canary. I imagined the Bergs' cat padding into the Anderssons' kitchen, knocking the cage off the table, reaching a paw through the broken door, pulling out the small yellow canary, already stunned from the fall, taking it in its jaws, between its sharp teeth, and prancing proudly out to the front yard. I imagined young Hansie witnessing the terrible carnage, paws batting the traumatized bird back and forth, feathers flapping in distress.

I called Hans a few days later to inquire as to the joy the new bird brought. "Oh, jeez," Hans said, "does he sing?! I'm gonna take him on the road. He just loves his cage, man. It's so big and beautiful. At night we cover him. The only thing he needs is a swing. He sings so much my wife shouts out, 'Enough!'"

"Is he red?"

"No, we just got the standard yellow, the one that sings the most. You shoulda seen all the colors they came in. There were brown and some kinda frosted colors. They were all singing at once. Oof da! What a concert. His voice is as good as Josh Groban's—man, he just sings all the time!"

Years later, after Mary died, Hans found another lovely partner to share his exuberant life. At their wedding, Ned Berg, considerably dwindled in stature, suffering from a wasting disease, approached me directly. I was certain I hadn't offended him lately.

"I want to say something to you," he started.

Oh-oh, I thought to myself. "Yes?" I said.

"Yes," he said. "I want to apologize. It's been thirty years I've had this on my mind, and it's long overdue. I'm sorry I threw dog shit on your steps."

"Really?" I said. "You did?"

"Yes. Don't you remember? I was kind of an ass."

I'd forgotten about that, but I remembered other things, none of which I related, and although I was tempted to bring them up, it seemed too back-alley. What I saw of him was his front—stooped, sad, fading.

"Of course," I said. "That's fine," I said. "I forgive you." We sat together that afternoon, celebrating the new marriage of our mutual friend Hans Andersson, whose beaming face said it all. We didn't talk much. It was good to listen to the band playing oldies, to watch the corny wedding videos of the children we used to know who now have children of their own, to sit with people from the old neighborhood, to guess how soon the new Anderssons would be selling the old house, and to hope Hans would still bring us krumkakes at Christmas.

Wolf Pups and Convicts

Dopamine lights up my brain in a beautiful, neon green, commanding me, Go fast! Immediately! In full throttle, my mind is a rich absinthe. Marshall's, on the other hand, is swaddled in caution, the color of calm cerulean, commanding him, Slow Down! Caution! Together, we are a Zen blend of aqua.

If left untethered, I spin out, pursuing all kinds of trouble, both terrifying and exhilarating. I'd be dead if it weren't for Marshall.

We've tried to follow our own rhythms in most things, especially when we hike across country and abroad. Sometimes my roaring impulses to conquer a mountain or chase a crazy dream demolish good sense. When he unleashes me alone, I return exhausted, delirious, glad to be home. After thirty plus years, he's taught me to settle for a "moderate" hike, despite my inclination to take a "strenuous" one.

While hiking the Loop Trail in the Cascades, tossing bulging handfuls of berries into my mouth, I offered Marshall a rich blend of blueberries, raspberries and salmonberries from my sticky hand. "Want some?" I said, striving to be generous.

"No, thanks," he said, leaning into his walking stick. "Might get giardia." He maneuvered around my little cache of berries assembled on the ground, and trod forward.

"Isn't it gorgeous? Aren't we lucky to be alone?" I was glad we hadn't run into streams of hikers, calves bulging under heavy packs. I dreaded children galloping around us, parents shouting warnings into the indifferent air.

"We're taking an easy hike today, right?" he said.

"Hey, check out my new boots!" I held up one dripping boot. "All muddy and no leaks!"

"Terrific boots," he said, sliding around sludge, rubbing his knee. He mopped his forehead with his handkerchief. "We there yet?"

The first few hours of hiking, tugging on his salt and pepper hair, he grappled with issues of home and work, fretting and stalling over dissatisfied clients, while I feverishly plotted our future adventure to Patagonia. Eventually, he trotted along in the present groove, cracking jokes.

He was happiest with short-term goals, so I announced the loss of a barrette. This allowed him to slow his pace in order to search and recover the lost item. He felt useful and I felt loved.

Rangers had directed us to the top of Larch Mountain loop where Mount Saint Helen, Rainier, Adams, Hood and Jefferson thrust up along the horizon like icy blue bubbles. Only a mile, and there it was. A fenced-in square at the top with a spectacular view.

"Awesome! Wow!"

"Heck, we coulda' stayed home and gone to the Science

Museum. Wouldn't have had to walk as far," he said, setting down his pack and stick.

"Look over there. Hood is magnificent. Listen! It's calling to us! Can you hear it?" I took out my camera, centered Mt. Hood in the lens and snapped the shutter. "How would you like a 12 by 16 of it right over our bed?"

Marshall sidled up close and slipped his hand under my shirt. "Which one is the North face?" He could veer off course easily.

I brushed his hand away with my elbow, reached down for my camera, backed up to the edge and snapped his photograph. "Cool!" I said. "Rugged!"

"Careful. You could fall off."

"Yup. Soaring thousands of feet rootless. What a rush!" I shivered.

"I need a nap," he said.

We found benches and stretched out, using our packs as pillows. Bright sun and damp piney fragrance lulled us. Marshall was soon snoring away while I watched tiny yellow, cloudless sulfur butterflies playing high altitude tag. Unbuttoning my shirt, I basked in the sun. It felt safe here. I imagined being weightless, floating off the edge, surrounded by nothing but sky.

Half an hour passed when the wind shifted. I was startled by the sound of low male voices—one a deep bass. A truck door slammed, then there was banging, metal against metal. Men's laughter.

I yawned, scratched my chest where the sun had begun its slow burn, and buttoned up my shirt. *So much for solitude and serenity.* Marshall was still lying on his pack, groggy.

"Did you hear that?" I said.

He checked his watch, looking for an answer. "Probably some men emptying garbage."

"Yuk. Other people's garbage," I said, remembering the first time I'd watched a homeless man eating from a dumpster behind a Dairy Queen.

"Not everyone has a choice," He sat up, leaned over to retie his boots and balance the load in his pack. Aging knees and bad feet slowed him.

A dozen men in florescent orange jumpsuits marched up the path toward us.

I'd seen men like these before. Teaching in prisons, a gauntlet of cellblocks. Hands strung through iron bars. Aching eyes. Clicking tongues. Moaning and kissing noises. Way inside me, a burning. Burning. My heart drumming or theirs?

I lowered my legs to the ground and got up. I walked up the slight ridge to the vista to admire the view again. Head down, I smoothed my shirt, avoiding eye contact. My nose filled with the rank smell of sweat. Heavy boots pressed into pliant earth.

"I went down, down, down, and the flames went higher..." sang someone. Nylon cloth swished between swinging arms and thighs.

A guy with long blond hair tied back into a ponytail paused behind me. I turned around and he leaned back, eclipsing the sun, scanning me from head to foot. "Hi," he said, in a low voice.

The other men bunched up behind and around him, making it impossible for Marshall to see what was going on.

"'Lo," I said, tugging and smoothing my hiking shorts. He pressed his steely legs against mine. I fought old impulses. Heat spread up my thighs. His breath was moist and close. Closing my eyes, I prayed *Back off! Back off!* My throat was burning with the taste of absinthe. My knees shook.

"Don't pretend you don't know me," he whispered. "I'm just like you." He stapled his eyes to mine, opening them wide. Then he winked. I felt dizzy, urging my body to reclaim its balance, but the hooks on my boots caught on his boots. I dared myself to raise my eyes to meet his.

"Marshall?" I said, my voice strangled.

"Marshall?" he mocked. I managed to unhook my boot. My throat froze, but my mind screamed, *Get away from me! Marshall? Can't you see what's going on?*

A guard moved rapidly up the path toward us, one hand poised over his gun, slung at the hip. "Move along, men," he said. The blond, mocking man took two steps back from me to lead the men back on track, single file. Head thrust forward rigidly on his neck, eyes trained, the guard nodded, silently counting men. "The taste of love is sweet when hearts like ours meet," he was singing. I loved Johnny Cash, and his was a damned good imitation. *Shit.*

"You all right, ma'am?" said the guard over his shoulder.

"Yes," I lied. I was able to make eye contact with my husband, and beckoned him over. He threw on his pack and came over to me.

"What's wrong?" He snapped the last buckle on his pack around his waist and shifted the weight around both shoulders, studying me. The men disappeared down the

"Those guys were totally scary and you weren't even looking."

"What are you talking about?" he said, yanking his backpack straps tighter.

"What's the difference? You failed to save me from possible rape and pillage."

He reached up to put his arm around me. "I don't get it. What the hell happened?"

I shrugged his arm off my back. I was lit up lime green. "If I were those guys, I would've shoved everyone into the outhouse, grabbed the car keys, and driven straight north to Canada."

Marshall put on his cap. "Y'know, that guard could've warned us."

"Right! He should post a sign. 'Hikers, beware! Prison cleanup crew!' Like those yellow tents that say, 'Wet floors!' Trouble is by the time you've seen them, you've fallen on your ass!"

"Just one little push over the canyon. Guts splattered all over the rocks. Bones picked clean." I went on. He leaned over to kiss me, smacked his tongue to his palette, tasting the sweetness of berries, and scratched his head. "I'm hungry. Ya' wanna eat here or down at that picnic area by the parking lot?"

"We can be seen better at the picnic area. It's a little closer to civilization," I said.

"Did I hear you right?"

We returned to the base of the trail. An elderly couple was climbing the stairs toward a picnic table. The man wore a straw hat, tilted jauntily at an angle, Hawaiian print shirt with bright red hibiscus blossoms on a blue background. Khaki trousers were belted under a round belly. His wife, face full of purpose, led the way in a peach colored dress, and carrying a white wicker picnic basket, big as a bassinet. By the time they reached the table, he was wheezing. She laid out a red and white checked oilcloth.

"How do you suppose she knew what size tablecloth to bring? Did she measure in advance?" I said.

When the old guy sat down, the woman pulled out bright yellow plastic plates and tableware. Next, she lined up phalanxes of covered food containers before her man.

"Bet she makes a mean potato salad," Marshall said, dumping his pack on the table a few yards away, wiping rain off the benches with his handkerchief.

"Are you kidding? She's got a five-course meal in that Tupperware."

"Should we tell them about the convicts?" he smiled, pulling out Baggies filled with cucumbers, oranges, cheese, crackers, and licorice.

"Maybe." With his pocket-knife, Marshall sliced cucumbers and cheese, lining them up next to the crackers in alternating rows. He peeled and segmented the oranges, placing them in a little wheel on a paper napkin between us. "The second-best thing to sex," he said, holding up a segment to my mouth.

"Beautiful presentation," I said, kissing him, studying the distance between our picnic table and the next.

From the corner of my eye, I observed the nearby couple, whose faces were lowered into prayer. "I may be interrupting their service, but I have to warn them." Before

Marshall could stop me, I bolted over to the other table, tripping over roots and rocks.

Pausing a few feet away, I shouted, "Some convicts on a cleanup crew are somewhere around here! Just thought you should know!"

"What, dear?" the woman looked up, her pale blue eyes moist and weary. She laid down her fork and screwed up her face.

The man examined me over the rim of his plate, which he held under his chin as he forked in mouthfuls of food. He scanned my berry-stained shirt, my short shorts, my muddy boots.

"Marshall?" I shouted. "Come and tell these nice people what's going on," I said, backing up a step or two.

"Doing great! You don't need me!" he shouted back.

"What does she mean by convicts, Mary?" said the man. "What sort of convicts?"

"I don't know. We saw them emptying garbage. They could be murderers or...pedophiles." I stepped forward and leaned into their faces. My voice was shaking. "But they're here in the campground. Thought you might want to know! Your lives could be in danger!"

The old man was digging into the Tupperware, building mounds of food onto his plate. Fried chicken, cold slaw, pickles, garlic toast, bacon. Mary smiled sweetly at me and shrugged her shoulders. I walked back to Marshall, plunking myself down next to him. I grabbed a few crackers, cheese, cucumbers, and all the remaining orange segments and shoved them into my mouth.

"They don't care," I said under my breath. "It's useless." My guts were tight and hard.

"I say we drive home. Lunch is over." Marshall said.

"She's got nerve, that girl! Bothering us with such trash. More o' that potato salad, Mary!" Mary's husband shouted.

"He's deaf," I said, staring at them. Mary glanced up at me, shook her head and turned away. The old man was hard at work, elbows flapping up and down like a predacious bird crawling over a carcass, shoveling forkfuls of potato salad into his mouth.

Suddenly, the old man spluttered and coughed. Little choking noises came out of his throat. His body jerked back and forth in spurts, an eating machine out of gear. His arms churned the air in wide, jerky circles. Mary, unable to speak, whimpered slightly, peered into his eyes, and began to pat his back. Her husband's chin was sunken into his chest. He had stopped flailing his arms, and his body was curling into itself like a large snail. He looked like he was going to burst.

Out of the bushes, down the path between the two picnic tables, streamed the work crew again. A few burly logger types, a couple of small ones, and the blond with the silky baritone, who brought up the rear, still singing "Bound by wild desire; I fell into a ring of fire..." He stopped mid phrase.

"Smells good, don't it?" he said to me, smirking, jerking his head toward the picnic feast. He fastened his eyes on mine. His upper lip lifted into a lewd curl.

I rushed back to Marshall and tugged at his shirt. "C'mon! The guy next door is choking to death!" I grabbed his fork, threw it down, and grabbed him by the hand. We stumbled over the fire grate, but recovered our footing. One of the cons, feet slapping flat on the ground like a duck, paddled sideways to get a closer look. The others clustered around in a loose knot. One with tattoos to his neck pulled a cigarette from his pocket, and clenched it between his teeth. A bookish man, glasses perched on the bridge of his nose, pulled a match from his pants pocket, lit it on his zipper and held it to the tip of the other man's cigarette, looking hard into his eyes.

"Think your ole man's got somethin' caught in his throat, lady," the blond guy offered, bulky arms hanging out from the sides of his body. He stared at the hibiscus man, clenching and unclenching his hands.

"Help us? Please?" Mary's voice was small and pleading. She was peering into her husband's face.

"Name's Sonny," the blond baritone said. Swiftly, he reached down and wrapped his beefy arms around the old man just under his rib cage.

The guard materialized, hand on his pistol, alert. "Whassup?"

"No trouble, officer, this older gentleman is choking! One of your men here is doing the whatchamacallit," Marshall said, stepping forward.

"...Heimlich Maneuver!" I whispered.

"Oh, zat all? We teach that. Case one of our men gets into trouble." The guard planted his feet squarely behind Sonny, hands on his hips.

I stepped behind Marshall, gripping his backpack carabiner with my index finger. His body blocked me from view. I steadied myself.

"I've got you!" he whispered over his shoulder. "No rape or pillage. Promise."

I peered around him to see what was going on.

Sonny balled his fists and pushed abruptly upward into the center of two hibiscus blossoms, just above the old man's swollen belly. He released and pushed again. A discernible chunk of chicken flew onto the end of Mary's nose and fell to the table with a little plop.

"Thank you!" she said, misty-eyed, picking up the piece of chicken and putting it in a napkin. "You saved my husband's life. God bless you. I don't care what you've done in the past. The Lord has blessed us today with the goodness of your soul Joe? Joe! How do you feel? Can you thank the nice man?"

Joe's pink color was returning. Sonny reached into the dirt under the picnic table and picked up the straw hat. He smacked it lightly against his leg, brushed off a few pine needles, and handed it back. Joe cleared his throat, turning the hat in his hands slowly, around and around.

Sonny made a joke to the tattooed guy. When he laughed, I noticed several teeth missing. He caught me looking at him, puckered his lips, and spat on the ground. The other men milled about, kicking the earth and scratching their bodies.

Joe, his voice ragged, burst out with religious fervor. "Have you accepted Jesus into your life, son? You can be forgiven. Jesus removes all sins. Here, take my Bible. You might be needing it. It's my way of thanking you and all." He motioned to Mary who reached into the basket, pulled out a small black book.

The guard intercepted, tipped his hat. "I'll keep it for him till we get back." He tucked it in his shirt and they all headed down the dirt path. The men, like trained dogs, followed him. I knew the balance between captor and captive could easily shift again easy as wind. Sonny glanced over his shoulder at me. Once more, I popped my head behind Marshall.

"I've had enough. Let's get out of here," Marshall said to me under his breath.

We packed up fast and hurried back to our car, throwing everything in back. We sped off, kicking up dirt and gravel.

"Marshall, slow up, we'll spin off the pavement!"

As he spiraled round and round down the mountain road, he reached over and grabbed my hand. "What exactly happened up there?"

"Nothing," I looked at him out of the corner of my eye.

"We could've stayed home and watched 'Orange is the New Black' on Netflix."

It was hard to stay mad at him. Besides, it happened so fast, he didn't see it coming. I couldn't describe it—too complicated. "You're ridiculous." I laughed. "I'm glad we left when we did."

"Our hike was over. Didn't seem smart to hang around. Those guys didn't seem any too safe."

I gratefully reached out to touch the hair that curled around his ears. Like tiny, silky coils made to spring back in place.

Something small appeared in the road ahead of us. Marshall slammed on the brakes.

"It's a wolf pup! She can't be more than a month old." The lowering sun lit up the tips of its fur. Its face was completely without guile. Round yellow eyes stared up at our big four-wheel drive vehicle. No alarm or fear on its face. No other wolves in sight. No siblings. No mother.

"Oh! Let's look at him." Tears sprang to my eyes. I cracked open the car door and prepared to jump out.

Marshall held me back by my arm. He smacked his other hand down on the steering wheel. "If you're thinking about taking the wolf home, forget about it! We already have three dogs, a cat and a snake. His mother is probably in the bushes somewhere. Whaddya gonna do? Go look for her too?"

I spoke softly to the cub, one leg in our car, one leg out. "Hi, little wolf. Oh, where is your mother? Are you alone? How will you eat? Do you know where to go? You're too young to be by yourself." The cub stood up and continued to stare at me before she scampered off into the woods.

"C'mon. Get back in. The wolf will learn to forage. You absolutely cannot take her." As soon as I closed the car door, Marshall pulled away and picked up speed.

"Okay, little wolf, goodbye." The lump in my throat hardened. "You're free." I wiped my nose with the back of my sticky hand. Marshall reached into his pocket and handed me his ever-ready handkerchief. He pulled his old maneuver to slide me closer to him, back in the day when there weren't seat belts—a fast left swerve of the steering wheel. Clever.

He slowed to thirty. The sun was almost gone. I squeezed my eyes shut.

"Don't look now, but guess who's following us?" he said, releasing my hand and gripping the wheel with both hands. I put my seat belt back on.

My head throbbed. I rubbed my eyes and glanced in the side view mirror. There, following close behind, was the white van.

"Who's driving?" I said.

"I don't know," he said. His voice shook a little. He kept his head up just over his fists, a race car driver, clutching the steering wheel, checking the rearview mirror.

"How'd they catch up?"

He sped up. The car rattled and vibrated. My head hit the roof of the car.

I became the wolf pup. Wandering in a forest. Steel trap. Searing pain. Blood gushing from my leg. Where is my mother?

I imagined myself prying open the steel trap. My hands torn, ragged and bleeding. Picking up the cub, holding her torn leg close under my arm. Staggering to the edge of the forest, to the freeway.

Sonny and the other men in orange surrounded me, jeering, punching the air with their fists, shouting. John and Mary tripped back to their car. Fell hard on the stones.

Then it was us. Caught!

I was half dreaming, half awake, sobbing. "Wolf cubs! Convicts! Joe! Mary! You! Me! Orphans! All of us!" Marshall reached for my hand and held it fast.

"Thank you," I said, my chin a beard of tears. "Thanks for coming with me on this crazy hike and for not letting me bring home a wolf pup."

The van overtook us. Gravel chinked at the sides of our car and snapped onto the hood. A tiny crack slithered across our windshield.

"Goddamn criminals, ruining my car," Marshall said, braking. We couldn't make out who was driving. Bent elbows, orange sleeves rolled up, hanging from open windows, bulging biceps, no faces. Fists pounding us to a pulp.

My head was oozing blood. And throbbing. I wiped it with his handkerchief.

"It was a good hike," Marshall said. "The mountains were spectacular. And your new boots—wow, they really held up!" Steering with his left arm, he tucked a lock of hair behind my ear. "You didn't lose anything else?"

Marshall's voice soothed me back to aqua. A calm envelope. "Nope. Don't think so."

He held my hand tighter in his lap. I interlocked my fingers, traced with blood, through his, in a prayer of gratitude. I stroked the whitening hairs that carpeted his wrist. He handled each curve skillfully one-handed. I felt a gentle swaying, like being rocked.

The Lamb Bash

"Uncle Merrill. You're looking fine this evening," teased Audrey.

Uncle Merrill was swaying in circles, supported by an extravagantly carved cane topped with a sterling silver parrot. His head was twirling like the ball on the end of a rope tied to a tetherball pole. He was trying to speak, to find something clever to say, but couldn't quite locate words.

"That's a nice stick you have there. Is it new?" Audrey was shouting now, her face reddening. Apparently, Merrill could neither hear nor understand.

"Watch," he said, peering out from caterpillar eyebrows over half-lidded eyes. He grasped the cane with one hand and, with immense concentration, unscrewed the parrot's head with the other hand. He proudly thrust the hollowed-out cane under his niece's nose.

"Ha-ha, Uncle Merrill! Is that a flask?"

"You betcha. I emptied it a few minutes ago. Pretty good, huh?" Uncle Merrill could barely stand.

"Great!" she said, grinning and turning on her heels to escort me, the interloper, into the dining room.

"I had no idea you two were relatives," I said. Uncle Merrill is known to be one of the wealthiest men in the country. Her connection to him shed new light on her own

entrepreneurialism, as well as her independence. It was further proof of the rumor that everyone around here is related in one way or another.

"Yes," she confided, "and the family drinks too much." We walked down the hallway in this, the oldest relic of upper-crust country-club life in the posh outskirts of Minneapolis. Interpersonal exchanges took place standing, drinks in hand. Dusty, satin draperies of a bilious green sagged from heavy brass rods; worn carpeting was a nondescript beige. Furniture was as old as its unwritten policy of WASP-only membership.

Calligraphed placecards, at the tip of each carefully placed knife, indicated the host's intent. My first clue about the formality of this occasion was the invitation we received six weeks in advance - an embossed invitation suitable for a wedding, requesting our presence at the "bash."

Harry was a new friend whom we'd met at another party. He was engaging, intelligent, funny. His technical savvy was far more up-to-date than mine. People who expand my world are likely to become treasured friends. In fact Marshall and I invited him and his spouse and several others to our home for a mid-winter dinner party. It went off like fireworks—explosions of laughter, vivid color, over in a flash.

I comforted myself in advance with the notion that at Harry's party, I would sit next to friends, or at least people I knew. No such luck. Marshall and I were clumped with a bunch of braggarts and weirdos, four men and one woman, at the losers' table. Marshall was seated across from me, too far away to be of consolation. Two empty seats next to me were for a couple who had decided, at the last minute, not to attend. Too bad. She was a childhood friend I would have enjoyed seeing again. I struggled through the first 15 minutes of dinner listening to tales of courtroom triumphs from a short, bald attorney named Richard, whose swollen face and be-ringed fingers showed nary a sign of hardship. His narrative of legal conquests carried me through a salad of baby greens, nuts, berries, and cheese. I checked the winners' table across the room. Audrey & Co. were hysterical with laughter and what I was sure were hilarious tales.

When Richard's tape wore down and a beautifully presented plate of rack of lamb, asparagus, and whipped potatoes arrived, he released me to the convoluted meanderings of a retired executive, Tom. Tom's uncombed, matted hair and crooked, slightly drooling mouth indicated he'd been dragged out of bed and hoped to return soon. Spots on his tie appeared to be historical discolorations. His sport jacket was rumpled, his tie, askew. I was afraid to look directly into his eyes, fearing what other signs of disturbance I might find. I focused on my food. The lamb was sublime, the asparagus delicate, the potatoes soft as a baby's bottom. The combination melted on my tongue as easily as a chocolate truffle. Tom's unintelligible commentary made little sense despite several start-overs. It was hard to find a second between his pauses to place word offerings at his altar where once, who knows, he might have directed thousands in his purview to meteoric heights.

By the third course Tom's wife noticed me and promptly patted the empty chair next to her, motioning for me to sit next to her. I was grateful to move out of earshot from the blowhard attorney and Snow White's dwarf Dopey's doppelganger. I looked at her fancily scrolled nametag: Martha, it said. *Of Mary and Martha, no doubt.*

"I heard you telling Richard that you're teaching at Drek School now instead of Dake," she began. "Why did you leave Dake?"

"Well, Martha, I like Drek because there's a kind of spiritual atmosphere there."

"Oh!" she squealed. "I'm so very glad to hear you say that! Ever since they replaced Dake's chapel with a library, I've been suspicious! They should have kept the chapel, don't you think?"

"But the new media center is beautiful, full of the latest technology. They preserved the wood paneling and stained-glass windows. They kept the old traditional atmosphere. In fact, I think they're showing reverence to education by filling it with tools of learning. Anyway, the media center is not the reason I left Dake."

"Reverence?" She furrowed her brow, which was otherwise smooth and untroubled.

"Yes, reverence for meditation and scholarship."

"But they didn't keep the cross. We need a cross."

"A cross? The school is supposed to be nondenominational."

"Yes. A big cross, made of raw wood, to remind us how Jesus suffered long and horribly. For us. And we should never forget it."

"Well, not everyone at the school believes that Jesus died for our sins. Or that he was the son of God, for that matter. Some people think he was just a guy—a prophet, a somewhat prescient prophet, but still…a guy."

"They certainly ought to believe. They'll be sorry come Judgment Day. I'm a true believer." She paused, then smiled, a glow of earnest pride radiating from her brow. She sighed and settled back into the chair. "I'm a fundamentalist Christian Republican."

"Really? Huh. I'm a left-wing Jewish Democrat!"

"Jewish? O-oooohhhhh! Well, God loves you." She patted me on the arm. The waiter brought a blue, frosted glass of fruit laced heavily with liqueur custard.

I dug in. "No kidding? How do you know that?"

"It's in the Bible, dear. God loves you." She patted me on the arm again. I put my arm in my lap, out of her reach.

"Funny, I don't have a picture of God as a person who loves or doesn't love certain people. I think of God as a spirit," I offered.

"Oh, no, dear. You're the chosen ones."

"Who? Chosen for what?" *Where was she going with this? If we were chosen, where did that leave her? How could she live with herself being unchosen? Was this her idea of humility?*

"All you Jews. You're special."

There it was. All you people. You're the special ones. So special you could ride the short bus for the handicapped. And we'll arrive in Scotland before ye. "I believe God includes everyone. Chooses everyone. You included," I replied. *I'm not letting her off that easy.*

"No. It's you and your people who have a special place in his heart. Tell all your friends."

What exactly is that special place? "All my friends?" I said.

"Yes, your Jewish friends. Be sure to let them know how special they are."

I poured her some water, planning an exit strategy. *God help me.* Uncle Merrill seemed to have lost his way to the men's room and was about to sit down at our table when Richard guided him by the elbow out the door. *God help us all.*

"And don't forget to let them know we're going to find Noah's Ark."

She isn't done with me yet. "Find Noah's Ark?" *What's that got to do with Jews being special? Is she planning some kind of reduction of our seed? Down to two of everyone. Perhaps a more practical approach...* "Don't you think Noah's Ark was made of wood?"

"Why, yes." Martha fluttered her eyelashes coyly.

"But then don't you think it might have smashed to smithereens on a big rock somewhere?" I smacked one palm against another to simulate loud slapping I've witnessed among Tibetan Buddhist monk initiates when they think they've reached a profound point of logic.

"Oh, no, the ark is still around."

Martha isn't buying it. "Where?"

"Only God knows. And God will decide when we're ready to see it again. It's proof of God's creation. But we're not ready for it yet. There are still too many folks who believe in evolution."

"You don't believe in evolution? No finches? No Darwin?"

"Work of the devil. Have you ever heard of a dog mating with a cat?" The corners of Martha's mouth turned down into a smirk and her lower jaw locked.

"No, can't say as I have." I was picturing the local tabby cat named Flo and Bernese Mountain Dog named Bubba engaged in copulation.

"There you go! Precisely my point!" She broke out in a beatific smile.

Maybe if I tossed the dice one more time. "Because a dog doesn't mate with a cat—that proves there's no evolution?"

"Of course! Don't you see? God created all creatures separate. If he'd meant for us to mate with apes, we'd be doing it. When was the last time you heard of a person and an ape having a baby?" Michael Jackson's chimp Bubbles came to mind.

"Humanoids and apes have common ancestry, but we evolved into different species. DNA reveals we have few genetic differences from apes," I ever so carefully articulated each word.

"Evolutionists dreamed up DNA to get rich."

I was truly stumped now. Yes, she told me, God loves everybody, so why shouldn't she? *Quite possibly our host had placed Martha and me at the same table as a malevolent joke. I refused to buy into his perversity. I would leave this dinner party with my dignity and my humor intact, lamb or no lamb.*

"I like that dress you have on," I expostulated.

"Yes, it's very old. I found it in my closet." Martha touched her collar and blushed a little. My ruse had worked.

"It looks like a Carole Little. I used to love that designer but she went out of business. *Girl talk. That's it.* "I love the colors she used," I went on. I released myself from the weight of responsibility to fix her. It dropped to the floor with a thud. *We can be friends for the next half hour and never recognize each other again, even if we're standing in the same line at the floral shop.*

"I don't know who that designer is," she said.

"It looks very nice on you. Carole Little designed clothes of motley colors and varying designs. Very playful. Sort of like Joseph's dreamcoat."

"Clothes like Joseph wore?"

"Yes. I think so. But I'm not sure Carole Little was thinking of that when she created the design of your dress," I said.

She smiled at me. "Look at the label." She reached behind her and held up the back of her dress at the neck. "What does it say?" she queried in a gesture of feminine conspiracy. *We were best friends now, bonding over a dress label.*

I peered at the label. "It says Joseph."

"No kidding?" She giggled.

"No, it's really Joseph's sister, Carole. Maybe you and he have something in common. Maybe you were chosen, not the Jews." *Oh-oh. Now I'm making light of a serious matter.*

"Only on the surface. My brothers are very good to me. My brothers would never cast me into the desert. We run a resort."

"Lucky for you."

"No. We're still one big happy family. One of our sons, Ned, married a Muslim girl, and we treat her just like she's one of us. At Christmas time we give her a present, just like we do for the others. At Easter, if she doesn't want to go to church, we don't push it or force her to go. Her breath gets just terrible when she fasts for Ramadan, but we don't hold it against her. I just keep my distance. Lucky they don't have any children yet, because I don't know how I'd feel about having my grandchildren praying on a napkin and facing East every few minutes."

"Mmmm," I said. "Dessert's wonderful, isn't it?"

"Yes, aren't we lucky to have such a feast?"

At another table Uncle Merrill scraped back his chair and wobbled to his feet.

"Like to make a 'nouncement! All hear this!"

The room of 50 or so guests hushed. Uncle Merrill had a reputation for bombast.

"Jes' lak to say our host outdid himself. Only thing was the lamb was undercooked! Raw. But I ate it anyway since it was free. So les' raise our glasses to the host. Bottoms up."

Stunned silence was followed by clinking of glasses and polite applause. Merrill miraculously reconnected his pendulous posterior to the chair.

Our host remained seated and boomed out with all the strength and kindness of a generous heart, "I have been told it's far better to serve lamb delicately cooked than too well done. I thank you for your attendance one and all."

More applause ensued. Long bars of moonlight streamed through the French doors, - striping the carpet. Time to go. I grasped Marshall's hand, thanked our host and passed Audrey and others who were in an uproar at a joke whose punchline we would never hear. Marshall and I made our way across the driveway, kicking up small stones, through the gauntlet of rosy-cheeked valets, whose crestfallen faces would perk up when the rest of the crowd called for their cars. Cutting through the grass, damp from sprinklers, I removed my shoes and ran, barefoot, into the easy soughing and heady green fragrance of pine. Voices faded away in the distance. Overhead, a screech owl sent its eerie trill into the cooling night.

Childhood Games

It started out fine. We fed Maggie's horses, stroking their velvet muzzles, cracking ice on top of the water tank, inhaling the rich blend of winter coats, hay and manure. At breakfast, we'd stoked away enough banana nut waffles to batten us down for our climb to the top, where we would eat again. In our backpacks, were tuna fish sandwiches, fruit, and chocolate.

As we were leaving Maggie's ranch house, Penelope picked up the pistol Maggie left lying by the sink, and turned it over in her palm, handling it like a string of pearls.

"Put it back. It's only for when I go out alone," Maggie said. "I've never had to kill anything. I just shoot it up in the air."

"Fine, Maggie, but you're not taking it along?" said Penelope, laying it slowly, reluctantly, back down.

"No, not today. They won't mess with us in a pack. They'll only take someone solo."

"Who's *they*?" I said.

"Oh, mountain lions...moose," Maggie said.

Penelope shrugged. "Oh, well. Live dangerously, I guess," she said.

"You're sure you don't need it?" I said, following closely on Maggie's heels. "I got pretty cozy with a grizzly in the

Rockies a few years ago. Brushed up against some big, fat hippopotami and lounging crocodiles in Kenya, too. Not that you asked, but swimming in the Indian Ocean, I ran into some very hungry sharks."

"What are you saying?" Maggie said.

"I'm saying I've been close enough to the edge, Maggie."

"We've got what we need. All set?" she patted her pack, and led us out the door to her car.

We parked our vehicle along the snowy shoulder of a road, close to a little summer cabin, nestled at the base of a steep hill.

"We'll be sitting on that cabin porch in a few hours, cooling our heels," Maggie said. "Let's go!" Her laughter sprinkled across our shoulders as we leaned over to tuck hand warmers into our mittens and snap on our skis. Thus, the four of us mounted our trek up the steep, snowy mountain trail. Today was to be a quiet conclusion to our annual week of downhill skiing, one last day in the Crazy Mountains, set aside for cross-country skiing, where the sun's face was rimming over a ridge, spreading fiery light through fir trees. Sunny stripes shot over the hills, turning white to bright yellow.

I wondered momentarily about our descent. "Let's ski conservatively," I said to Maggie quietly, "since for your fly fishing trip to Mexico and my trip to the Galapagos, we need all limbs intact."

"Right. I'm with you!" Maggie said.

Upward we pressed, one ski in front of another, through magnificent, tall trees. I'm the only one living at sea level and don't adjust quickly to the altitude. As we ascended, my breath sped up. The rest of the group was full of energy, and I detest being the slow one, the last one, or the liability, so I pushed through it.

An unwritten rule of our little group is "Keep up or drop out."

Deepok Chakra, the world's current authority on diet, breathing, and blood type, advises not to breathe too hard during exercise. It makes sense in theory, but our group's pace forced me to move beyond Chakra's judgment.

"Did you know women ranchers are among the highest percentage of women CEOs in the country?" Maggie said to Karen.

"Great to know, but where are they at calving time?" Karen said. "I could use a few extra hands at roundup."

My three skiing companions and I are childhood friends, still playing childhood games with the same old rules. We've skied together for years. Now in our mid sixties, we've advanced from "playing" horse: Karen and her partner run a flourishing Arabian stud ranch. Maggie, a divorcee, maintains her cattle ranch nearby and cares for her elderly father, who bought the acreage originally. When it's time for her to corral new calves for auction, Karen brings in hands to help—women helping women. Penelope, who used to "play" banker, now owns a bank in New York. We used to "play" school, and I've spent a lifetime in academia. We've worked hard, grown older, and stayed strong, despite the usual dying friends and relatives, unemployed children, surgeries, and a sucking sense of duty. Maggie has declared our gathering a "no groan zone," and so it is. We bully gravity, staring and daring it down.

I kept skiing along, marching like a foot-soldier, up, up, up. Left, right, slide. Left, right, slide. My skis were slipping backward down the hill. Maggie and Karen's skis were shorter and easier to handle than my waxless, longer ones.

Though I was dying to rest my eyes on the meringue-covered hills, spruce limbs laced with heavy snow, and bright, blue sky, I was forced to focus on my skis. After more than an hour, I was ready to step out of line.

"Take little steps," Maggie advised. "We're almost at the top!"

"Great!" I said, hungry for lunch. Soon there'd be an end to this heart-pounding huffing and puffing. As we climbed, I was reminded of our playground game Captain, May I? I almost asked her, "Giant or baby steps?"

The aim of Captain, May I? was to reach a certain goal by taking small or big steps. Captaincy belonged to whoever seized it with the most premeditation, talent and élan. The captain issued orders to take a certain type, number, and direction of steps. We followed her directions, asking first, "Captain, May I?" If we forgot the magic phrase, the captain could send us reeling backward. Even if we used all the right words and the captain granted our request, we were still at her mercy. Whoever was captain wasn't obliged to be fair. She could forbid us from moving, regardless of etiquette or equity, and exercise favoritism without forfeit. Whoever got to goal first was captain.

We used specific adjectives to describe the types of steps we wanted to take, developing linguistic imagination for the purpose of entertaining and persuading the Captain. "Big" and "little" wouldn't quite do for some captains. I tried big words such as "colossal" and "miniscule" for effect. Groveling helped, of course. But not too much. "Pretty please with sugar and cream on top" was a useful expression. "Please, please, please, oh, please," was overdoing it.

Years ago, Karen was captain for the longest. When she was captain, we could move just a few baby steps in five minutes, depending on the length of recess. Maggie often forgot what she had just promised and decreed liberal judgments on everyone. Penelope was so busy counting out the steps and calculating how long it would take for us to reach goal, she, too, was captain relatively briefly. I was more concerned with the words my friends used to describe than the types of steps they wanted to take. In Captain May I, we learned courtesy, vocabulary, respect, humility, and the subjective nature of power.

Another, less civilized, game we played was King or Queen on the Hill. Whoever arrived first at the top of a hill, staked her claim, "I'm queen!" The object was to remain queen as long as possible. The second she arrived on top, our assault against her began. Shoving, pushing, kicking, any means of brute force to that end, were legal. Insinuation, undermining, sneering—getting her to laugh or cry—were also legal. The biggest, bravest girl, the one with the longest arms or the loudest mouth, was queen the longest. From this game, we learned rules of the street and of corporate America.

On our ski tour, today, Maggie's leadership was automatic, due to her familiarity with the territory, but she kept stopping to tell stories. When I thought we were at the top, it turns out we had arrived at just one more mound in a series of peaks that went on and on.

We didn't ask permission. We took whatever steps we wished—sidestep, herring-bone, or a combination of the two. Sidestepping was tricky because the path was narrow and steep. With long skis, I teeter-tottered on the ridge of several steep switchbacks. Looking down a snowy precipice, at a path I'd just side-stepped, was harrowing, so I alternated with herringbones. My legs grew tired, my breath was labored, and I paused frequently. Those behind me were forced to stop as often as I did. Although they didn't comment, I sensed my pace was too slow.

Finally, Maggie said, "You know, I've only been to this picnic ground once before. If someone wants to lead, go ahead." Karen was itchy to speed ahead, so we reverted to a modified King on the Hill. Maggie simply stepped aside for Karen to lead us. We were, after all, a smidge older, prone to mixing up our games, with well-defended feelings and behaviors.

Eventually, Karen turned and waited for Penelope to take over. Since we paid lip service to democratic principles, it was declared time for me to lead. I relished sculpting fresh tracks, stealing an occasional quick peek at the hundreds of spruce saplings, their tops bent over from shrouds of snow, like old women, their trunks still bursting with vitality. When I could manage a few seconds, I gaped at the tops of full-grown fir, laden with the bulk of newly fallen snow. No signs of felines, just an occasional scrub jay, cawing.

Finally, at a plateau, Maggie peered in all directions and relented that there didn't seem to be any "top" to our climb. "I don't see the picnic ground, but let's keep on. I'm not sure which trail we should take down."

No one objected, at least not aloud.

"Let's find a spot to sit down," Karen said, sliding back into a path. We skied down and around switchbacks for another half hour or so.

"I think I know the place," Maggie said.

We arrived at a stream, littered with fallen timber. Maggie stopped to examine tracks. We were forced to ski back and forth across the stream, balancing on icy logs, with millimeters to spare on either side of us.

Some paw prints were small, round punctures in the crust, and some were long, almost human. "Are there two animals?" I asked her.

"No, the long tracks are where she was stretching out her forelegs to jump," Maggie said.

I pictured a mountain lion, gracefully extending her long legs across the streamlet. I noted many fresh trails, suggesting more than one cat, despite Maggie's opinion.

"You're not sorry you didn't bring your gun, right?" I asked Maggie. Maggie said nothing. "I thought we were going to stop for lunch," I said. Maggie said nothing. Maybe I misunderstood the rules. Or maybe there were no rules.

"Let's stop, you guys. Karen!" I said. Karen didn't answer. We clambered over a few more logs and forded the stream again. I checked my watch. Maybe everyone was too cold to speak.

"All right, it's two o'clock," I said to no one in particular. "Since there's no picnic ground, let's just stop and eat here!" I said.

"I'm sorry. I kept thinking I'd find the picnic spot, but I'm turned around," Maggie said. "We probably should stop. It's getting late." We stopped in our tracks, plunked our packs down, and gobbled up our lunch, without ceremony, standing up. The stream snaked around us, black and wild.

Snow was falling, forming clumps around us. I had a chance to drink in the deep, sharp valleys and tall trees, covered with heavy, white shawls. It was definitely worth the haul. We were all shivering from wet clothes, evaporating perspiration, and cold lunch. "How much farther?" I asked, chewing the last of my sandwich.

"We're definitely more than halfway," Maggie said.

"Only half way?!" I said, trying not to sound alarmed.

"We're standing right in the very spot where a mountain biker guy I know was attacked. He was looking around at the view, ready to go back down. His heart was pounding so loud, he couldn't hear anything except the rushing river. All of a sudden, a mountain lion was on him, clawing down his back, biting into his neck."

A glob of tuna fish stuck in my throat. "So what happened?"

"He lifted his bike over his head and smacked the lion with it."

"Amazing," Penelope said.

"True story," said Maggie. "The lion was dazed by the bike long enough for the guy to get his bearings. Just then, some noise distracted the lion, and he leapt away through the trees."

"So the guy got away?" Karen said.

"Came home, and yeah, he was fine."

"What about moose? Seen any of those?" I asked.

"Never seen one, but you gotta watch out for them. They'll trample you with their front hooves," Maggie said, smiling.

I examined the tracks in the snow. She stared at me. She reached into her pocket and held out a tissue. "Did you know your nose was bleeding?"

"No, but I'm not surprised. It's the altitude."

"Better not get too far behind," said Penelope. "Blood has a powerful scent."

"Not funny," I said, with a sudden cold shiver that started at the base of my spine and crawled up behind my ears.

"I'll go behind you," said Penelope, stepping out of line to follow me.

"Here we go," said Karen, shoving her reddened hands back into her mitts. We closed up our packs and proceeded. Karen led out, then Maggie. Then me, with Penelope last.

"Most people look out at the trail ahead," Maggie said to me. "I look up at the tops of trees."

I scanned the trees. Not a whisker.

Maggie was on a roll. "Some friends of ours were skiing here a month ago and stopped to take a bunch of pictures of each other. When they developed their pictures, there was a big lion in a tree branch hanging right over their shoulders."

I was feeling claws and fangs in my neck. "I'm glad I'm not last. All creatures pick the one who's bleeding or last," I said.

"We're close to the end. At the bottom of this hill is the little cabin we saw when we began. See it?" Maggie pointed to what was the longest valley of ice crust I'd ever seen. In fact, it was a series of sloping rills that looked as glossy as a skating rink. "Then we'll drive home," Maggie said, a note of promise in her voice.

Karen was already descending, slicing into the dense crust, piercing the ice with her poles, whooping. Penelope looked at me, her eyebrows knotted into a query.

"Go around me. I'll catch up," I said. I studied Penelope's hopping traverse. There was absolutely no way I could copy either woman's style. Walking down was not an option. I could do this. I would do this. After all, we're all downhill skiers. This was nothing. Just a little ice.

Maggie looked me up and down. "Try the pole squat," she said, demonstrating. "Watch!" she shouted, as she made an ess curve down the hill. "Follow me!" Maggie shouted over her shoulder, laughing. It looked like the position slalom racers take, except slalom racers don't squat on top of their poles, they keep them by their sides.

The rounded squat reminded me of Shoot the Duck, an old ice skating trick we did at the school rink, where we hunkered down, arms forward, stuck out one leg, and skated for as long as we could on one skate, balancing. It was my favorite trick, transforming me instantly into a skating star. I hadn't tried it in a while, not counting the decades.

There's an important difference between Shoot the Duck and Pole Squat. Ski poles are not involved in Shoot the Duck. At the same time as Maggie straddled her poles, she manipulated them up and down between her legs, using them as a rudder. Sexy.

What made me try it had nothing to do with logic. It had to do with the sheer exhilaration of trying something new. "Here I go!" I shouted to no one in particular, since the other women were already far down the valley, including Maggie. Forgotten was the promise Maggie and I made. Forgotten was any form of fear. Forgotten was that it may not have been the best time to launch my debut. Forgotten was the fact that once begun, I couldn't change my mind. It's not the first time I've hurled myself headlong into situations and weighed the consequences afterward.

Besides, it looked like fun.

Actually, I had a certain four-legged feline in mind. I was the last one again and my nose was still bleeding. S/he who snoozes, loses. Down I went, squatting on my poles, feeling awkward and wobbly. Once I was on my way down, I realized I couldn't stand up. It was a treacherous plane. Midway down the first hill, I was out of control.

My body, skis and poles were not one. I was descending an icy slope, against my will, too fast. Down, down, still squatting on my poles, trying to catch up to the other three women, who were well ahead of me.

My skis were headed straight down the hill as I tried to hunker over them, reaching my arms out the way I did in Shoot the Duck, but this terrain wasn't flat like a skating rink, and my torso was leaning back. The snow crust was thick, and I couldn't press my poles down through the skin of the ice at this angle. There was no way in hell I could traverse or stop. Over one ridge and down to the next. I exerted every ounce of strength I had in my quads.

Just before I reached the last hill, I realized what a dumb idea this was. What the hell was I thinking? Before I reached the bottom of the last, long hill, I folded my right leg under me, a deliberate act to stop my crazy luge-like recline. Both feet twisted at an abnormal angle. My left leg shot out in front. Trying to twist my body back into human shape, I rolled over onto one pole, bending it under me. I collapsed onto my side into a contorted heap, several yards from the bottom of the last hill. At least, I wasn't moving anymore.

"Are you all right?" Penelope shouted. There the three of them sat, on the cabin porch, stretched out, skis off, boots up on the porch rails, faces toward the setting sun, eyes closed.

"Fine!" I shouted back, peering down the hill at them. I stumbled as fast as I could to my feet, feeling both feet, an excellent sign. My left knee was not happy. I undid my skis and rolled onto all fours. I gathered both skis, laced my poles around my wrists and punched through the crust, dragging my ski tips and poles behind, pain shooting up my left leg, watching the sun lower in the sky, wondering how long it would take me to get to the bottom. I was trudging slowly, inches at a time. I scanned the trees, up and down.

Punch, punch. Punch, punch. This was the tranquility promised. The restful conclusion. I sat back down again. It was too far. I packed snow around my knee, then lay on my back. The ice felt good.

"You sure you're all right?" Penelope shouted from her perch.

"Just resting!" I shouted back, peering at them, pissed. *For ye suffer fools gladly, seeing ye yourselves are wise,* suddenly made sense.

"Come and have an orange with us," said Karen.

"No, thanks!" I said.

Penelope clambered out of her chair to bring me a section of orange. I gobbled it down with a dose of self-pity. She knelt down and peered into my face. "What's going on?" I could've told her the truth, that I was tired and pissed off, that my knee hurt like hell, that it wasn't relaxing, however beautiful, but I couldn't. I just couldn't.

"Nothing," I said. "Just winded." Part of the rules of the game. Act tough when you feel like shit.

It was a short hike back to the car. Everyone skied but me. I was trying to hide a limp. Maggie slowed down next to me and looked me closely in the eyes.

"Godddamn, sonofabitch," I said. "I fucked up."

"I'll carry your skis," she said, and she did, hoisting my skis and poles over her shoulder, the bent one sticking up, broken.

"I didn't get eaten!" I smiled at Maggie. I didn't mind bringing up the rear this time. I was thinking about how I'd manage on the Galapagos lava.

We got to the truck, and Maggie patted the seat in front next to her, looking at me. Penelope and Karen climbed in the back. No one mentioned my fall. I turned my seat heater to high, tears of pain stinging my eyes. I glanced for one final time along the edges of the road, into the branches of a Doug fir, for signs of life. Sure enough, there she was, a sinuous, muscular golden body, slung over the crotch of a lower branch, face more cunning than the stuffed toys we used to pile on the pillows of our chenille bedspreads. She flicked her tail, twitched the tawny tufts inside one perked-up ear, narrowed her eyes, and ran her long tongue across her upper lip, flattening her whiskers.

"Great day to be alive," I said.

"Next?" said Maggie, negotiating the curve in the road.

Why I Fight with Bobbie But Not Billie

I was feeling happy to see Billie, but not Bobbie. Billie's the one who helped me get kicked out of the private school I hated. We smoked outside the building, cut class, and acted as bad as we could, at least by 1950s standards. We had good chemistry, still do. Bobbie and I, on the other hand, fought like back-alley cats.

When we were eight years old, Bobbie and I kicked, bit, snarled, and scratched. Our battles were ferocious. We left tiny, purple fingernail moons on each other's forearms. I got so hot, my face turned crimson and splotchy. Once, when I fainted, the nurse thought I had scarlet fever and sent me home with my father. At least that's what she said, although now I think she wanted to get rid of me. I don't know. And that's okay with me. It's okay not to know.

Billie lives in San Francisco, so when she called to say she'd be in town and we could meet for lunch, I was happy—that is, until she told me she'd included her twin sister in our plans. Even though Bobbie lives in town, we don't see each other. I didn't want to hurt her feelings, so I didn't object, but I knew our date was doomed to fail.

The first bad omen was that Bobbie gave me the wrong directions to her house. I'd forgotten to bring her phone

number, so I couldn't call her. By the time I found her building, I'd wasted 15 minutes following her detailed email directions. But I knew better than to challenge her. She wrote, "Take a right after Nye's and then circle the block, crossing the street at the T and heading up the driveway to our apartment building." Actually I needed to take a right *before* Nyes, not *after,* which I figured out after I circled the block and ran into a one way going the wrong way, leading me away from rather than to her house. I had thought, *Oh, she must know the directions. She's lived there for decades and knows how to give directions.* I forgot about the fallibility of absolute certainty.

The second bad omen was my memory that Bobbie has to be right. Always. So, I went my own way and found her place, using logic. When I picked the two women up, I said, "Sorry I'm late. I get lost really easily these days. Must be our age." I hate that in myself, when I demur to others because I don't want to hurt their feelings, when I fall back on the handy "my memory is failing me" excuse, when I'm actually the one who's put out.

The third bad omen was that as soon as Billie and I hugged one another, and the two of them got into the car— Billie in front, Bobbie in back—Bobbie leaned over the front seat and asked, "So, what have you been up to?" I didn't even have time to take a breath.

It's a rather large question to answer in a car ride you know is going to be about two minutes long, especially since Bobbie's snapping black eyes looked like she could blast and peel the skin right off my organs. She was an emotional dead ringer for Gunther von Hagens, the guy who started Body Worlds. She was Guantanamo without the big round light, not exactly the type to inspire one to divulge one's secret life. Anything more than a perfunctory, "Oh, nothing much," would be suicide.

Billie was looking at me with a benign Buddhalike expression, laced with a slight, ironic lip curl. Billie's eyes are aquamarine, their facets sparkling. Since I'd seen her last, she'd figured something out. It felt important to be nice to Bobbie since they are twins, after all, and blood is thicker than water.

The difference between them, however, is like the difference between a butterfly and a buzzard, Billie being the butterfly. Aside from the typical kinds of sibling similarities like voice quality, accent and general shared interests, their approach to life is not in the same class, genus or species.

Fortunately, by the time I processed all this, we were at our lunch spot. It was pouring rain.

Billie and Bobbie slogged through mudpuddles in sensible Rockport hiking shoes, while I dodged them in red leather Nike loafers. The twins wore hooded raincoats, but I hadn't bothered since I figured the parking and restaurant would be an in and out sorta deal. When we got inside, I was chilled and dripping.

No sooner did we sit down at a table, than a perky little woman on a mission came over with a strip of stickers that said "I Ate" on them, like the ones you get after you vote or go to the doctor's office.

She grinned and cocked her head. "Did you know today is the day all restaurants are participating in a big AIDS drive? Part of your bill will be sent to the cause."

"Oh, great," said Billie and Bobbie in unison. I said nothing because I'm tired of AIDs drives. There are a lot of sicknesses and AIDS never was my favorite. I don't like cancer bracelets either. Or ribbons for cancer. There's a different colored bracelet or ribbon for breast cancer, pancreatic cancer, leukemia, AIDS, brain cancer, supporting the troops in Iraq, and just about every other kind of blight, so the world can know you either have AIDS or cancer or a child in the war or you care a lot about someone else who does and that you are a generous, compassionate person who spends money on those less fortunate, even if it's you. It's a fashion statement. Even the stars and starlets at the Academy Awards wear them with their diamonds and sequins. The little woman counted out enough stickers and envelopes and information brochures for four people and dumped them on our table as if we ought to be expecting someone else, maybe a man, or carrying the message to someone else, like good

Samaritans, and we all smiled at her and nodded as she wandered off to the next table.

At the top rung of the ladder of the great philosopher Maimonides' Ladder of Charity is the person who gives anonymously without being asked and doesn't tell anyone. At the bottom rung is the person who is asked and then gives and tells everyone else about it. If you are asked and show it off on a daily basis by wearing a bracelet or a ribbon, I figure that's a sub-rung on the Ladder.

Bobbie continued her fusillade of questions. "So, what are you writing these days? What kinds of things? Have you thought about self-publishing? I know of some great places. One of my friends…"

Billie went undercover and said, "While you two are talking, I'm going to read the last two pages of this book so I can give it to you." It was a summer-reading book with a bikini-clad blonde on the cover, but a free book is a free book, so I said yes. She finished it up in just about one minute and placed it perfectly parallel to my napkin. That's the kind of person she is. She's kind. She's smart. She's exacting. She's tidy. She follows through. I don't need for her to wear a ribbon or a bracelet to know that.

I felt obliged to hold up two-thirds of the conversation, since Billie seemed to have turned passive in the years since we were friends. Both twins are birders, so I started out with what I thought was a tribute to the enigma of the spheres, an unanswerable query, a paen to mystery. I love mystery. I love waking on an April morning, not knowing if I'll smell damp spring snow, a heady, humid bursting of green, or the faint scent of lilacs.

"There have been huge flocks of mergansers and loons at Lake Harriet over the past month..." I began, humbly, slightly stumbling...

Bobbie interrupted, "Oh, yes, I saw some over at Diamond Lake. There were Hooded Mergansers, Common Mergansers, Red-Breasted Mergansers, Grebes, Goldeneyes, Buffleheads..."

"Yes, yes, I know. I saw them," I said. "I saw the mergansers and the grebes and the buffleheads. As I was about to mention, the newspaper said a huge number of loons stopped here last week, more than in past years. They said it was because the ice is breaking up later than usual up North."

"Yes," Bobbie said, and opened her mouth to speak again. I wanted to finish my thought. "So, anyway, here's what's on my mind," I asserted. "It's really interesting to think about how birds know the ice hasn't broken up. How do you think they know that? Do they send up scouts to the north and then wait for them to come back before they finish their summer migration?"

"Oh, that's easy," said Bobbie breathlessly. "One of them stops at a city lake and then they all stop. They follow the flock. Just like how a decoy works for hunters. One spots the decoy, heads for it, and the others follow." Bobbie gave a wry smile, punctuated by a kind of pursing of her lips, to suggest no further discussion was necessary. Billie was mute.

"No," I said, "that's not what I meant. My question isn't how or why they cluster together. My question is 'How do they communicate to one another? Do you think there's a pilot duck? Who figures it out and tells the others?'"

Bobbie scoffed, "Oh, the trouble with people is they're always anthropomorphizing animals. Loons don't tell each other anything! They're conditioned through instinct."

"Wait a minute," I said. "Isn't instinct memory? Isn't memory learning? They must learn from each other. They must talk."

"No, they're two different things entirely. We have free will and birds have instinct. It's evolutionary." She smiled at her sister as if they had an inside joke on me.

"Would you like some of my Moroccan tart? It's delicious," Billie said.

"Yes, I would," I said, and she cut me a small bite and put it on my plate. It was a gift from God, truly magnificent food, sweet and savory at the same time. I rolled it around with my tongue, humming happily to myself.

Bobbie said, "I'll have some too," and stuck a knife and fork into her sister's plate to cut off a big wedge.

Maybe it was Bobbie's predacious tendencies. Maybe I was jealous of the amount of tart she got. For whatever reason, I was compelled to carry on what had taken a turn for the worse, despite what I figured was the inevitable demise of all inquiry. "I just read a National Geographic feature about how we underestimate the learning and memory of animals. Like my dogs, for example. One of them is terrified to walk on the North side of the lake because of the sound of the train. Once I took him too close to a train and he freaked out. He's been terrified of trains ever since. He stops dead when we go toward the train and refuses to move."

"That's just conditioning," Bobbie said. "You can recondition him to go if you want to. Just pull him."

"It doesn't work," I said, sticking my neck out further. "He's thirteen years old and we have two other dogs. If I pulled him forward, I'd break his legs. Besides he has degenerative disk disease and pulling hurts his neck quite a bit. Anyway, my point is, his fear is based on memory."

"No it isn't!" said Bobbie, lowering the guillotine, the one she keeps on hand for incorrect phraseology, or worse, foolish thinking. "Get him a harness. You can recondition him."

"We have a harness, Bobbie. It doesn't work. Speaking of birds and memory," I said, remembering from years ago that when she perseverates, it's best to redirect her. "We have two Mallard hens who have come for four years to our front planter beds and last year one of them had her nest raided by raccoons. It was awful…"

Bobbie interjected, "Everyone has to eat!" She shrugged her shoulders and showed her teeth for her sister. They smirked at each other.

I'd like to have shown her the eggs with half formed and partially digested ducklings. I wish our waitress had served it to her as a side dish, creamed. I wish she'd seen the little feet curled up inside the shell. I wish she'd witnessed the look in the hen's eye when she exploded out of her cover, like a torpedo, dropping feathers and guano in a mad panic.

"But, my point is, that particular hen didn't come back this year and the other one did. She remembered her bad experience," I said, "and was smart enough not to repeat it."

Both twins laughed. "Ha, ha!" they mocked. The scientists. When they were together, they colluded as only those genetically related can. I was unhappy that Billie and I weren't having this conversation, just the two of us. It wouldn't have been a contest over the orts of opposing points of view. It would have been an even exchange, a kind of tacit agreement, even if we disagreed. We established this truce eons ago.

Bobbie started a new narrative. Evidently I hadn't learned enough. "Did you know loons have different calls which mean different things? I have a tape that explains all the different calls of loons, for example. You could get the tape if you wanted it. I can't remember the name of it. There's a territory call and a mating call…"

How stupid did she think I was? She was still back in Elementary Loon and I'd completed Advanced. "I know many of their calls," I said. "I hear them nightly at our cabin. As a matter of fact, I do loon calls."

They both stopped eating and stared at me, their forks in midair. "You do?" said Billie.

"Yes, in fact if I did one here, the whole restaurant would get quiet."

Billie laughed. I laughed. I threw back my head and was about to let go of a beautiful trilling call, but stopped, deciding to keep it private. In retrospect, it might have proved my profound understanding of ornithology, once and for all, and might have put an end to Bobbie's need to drive home her line of pure reasoning. But I refused to *put an antic disposition on.* I didn't feel desperate enough.

What Bobbie and I would probably never see eye to eye about was that different loon calls are a kind of talking. She applied the usual nomenclature to loon calls, naming one a

94

tremolo, one a hoot, etc., but she refused to accept the term "communicating."

All this arguing was turning my kishkes. It hadn't been an intellectual exchange. It was a game of Dominate and Win.

I had a question, which I kept to myself: *How can any human being be so self-important that s/he or believes his/her line of thinking is The Truth,* especially when it comes to animal behavior. Scientific theory changes constantly. Only recently have humans discovered the immense complexity of the language of whales, for example. Each creature has its own individual song that carries up to hundreds of miles through the sea, maybe further.

With Bobbie present, I had about a tenth the fun. But it was my fault. I knew too well what I was getting into. When the waitress came with the bill, each one of us tried to pay. Since I was closer to the waitress, I insisted harder and closer and I won. What a triumph. I got to pay the bill for The Lunch of Argument. I won the battle and lost the war. Now I was out my hard-earned serenity and $38 dollars.

Billie and I had barely uttered two sentences to each other. In an effort to be polite, I didn't follow my better instincts and cheated myself out of a chance to talk to Billie. I really wanted to be just with her. I should have insisted. The rain had slowed to a drip. Still damp, and now unhappy, I dropped the twin scientists off at the door, glad to be done with lunch.

I emailed Billie and tried to explain why next time I wanted to meet her for lunch without her twin. She confided that when they were growing up, her sister was the one who got all the attention at the dinner table, and that she had simply learned to defer to her to preserve the peace. But, she said, she'd know better next time we met.

Even at my age, which is almost 65, I'm still learning technique.

It's tough to be human. Maybe it would be easier if we three were born loons. Billie and I would sniff the air, and light out for the Northern Territory, without looking back, up the flyway to Park Rapids. If the ice were still thick, we'd drop tail and stay there, leaving Bobbie back in Minneapolis, letting her rely on her own sweet, perfect instincts.

Harold In His Boxer Shorts

"Go get a bathrobe, Harold. It's unappetizing, your coming down to breakfast, day after day, seeing you in your boxers. Do you want our children to grow up like you, eating breakfast in their underwear?"

"We don't have any children," Harold said, hoping she'd fix his soft boiled eggs.

"Of course not. And why is that?" Betty said.

"Because I wear boxers to breakfast?"

"No, because you don't understand the art of ceremony. Every morning I set the table with cloth napkins and linen place mats and you come to breakfast half naked and eat over the sink. All I ask for is a little decorum..." Tiny drops of saliva spattered Betty's pink satin bathrobe. A vein on her right temple pulsed. Harold's mother, whose six sons ate in shifts off a plastic Myrtle Beach tablecloth before they ran off to football practice, hadn't taught Harold proper etiquette.

"But, Betty, you always complain that my heavy bathrobe jams the washing machine. If I get dressed, I spill on my tie. This way we conserve energy."

Harold never gave up.

"At least put on clean underwear. You slept in those."

"I'll take a shower after you do. Besides, Betty, dear, how would you know what I slept in?" Harold took a step toward Betty, who backed away.

"That's it! Get your own goddamned breakfast. Fetch the paper yourself. I hereby resign as your maid. I'm getting ready for work." Alex, the Airedale, cowered and slunk out of the room.

Harold looked puzzled. He studied the hair on his chest. It was turning a soft shade of gray, like fog, between his sagging pectoral muscles. How soon until it was all white like the alter kockers at the health club? What color would his father's chest hair have been if he'd lived, may he rest in peace? Silver? White?

Maybe he shouldn't have married so late in life. Living alone, he did what he wanted. Living with Betty was one ultimatum after another: a split-level ranch home next to a quiet little church. A dog, and now—kids. He was trying, god knows.

Harold missed living in the city. In the city, he could go to the museum, night or day, and visit his old favorites, like the Robert Indiana poster that said "Eat/Die." In this complicated world, he appreciated someone who could clearly sum up life. He loved its bright finality. And then there was the one by Lichtenstein, the pop artist, of a blonde woman with a very pained expression on her face. Above her gaping mouth was a string of bubbles and a word balloon with the regret, "Ohmigod! I forgot to have children!" Harold knew it was supposed to be funny, but it always made him cry. He didn't want to forget. Betty had her heart set on the right things.

What was he doing wrong? Was he shooting blanks? Would God ever grant him children? Wasn't he deserving?

He stumbled to the cupboard and found the right size bowl to microwave his soft boiled eggs. Was it two minutes, three minutes or six? He couldn't remember. He pushed Easy Minute five times. He reached into the drawer and grabbed the largest knife he could find to slice a bagel.

He hadn't slept well. Life was out of control. Too much to do. Too much to think about. He should have stayed in bed a few minutes longer to avoid Betty's meshuggeneh morning tirade. Resentful of her role as personal shopper for women whose lives were too busy to juggle children and jobs and used her to paw through racks of clothing to find just the right outfit to wear to $1,000 a plate benefit, Betty was tired of serving others. She had no respect for her profession which he suggested she consider a genuine contribution to humanity.

After all, Harold was tired too. One of the city's huge team of defense attorneys, he no longer believed in his job. He dreaded angry voice mails, piles of paper stacked up on his desk, scores of phone numbers on his tapped-out pager, and his assistant's multi-colored post-it notes indicating degree of urgency. Sincerity bugged him, especially from altruists. Every response plunged taxpayers deeper in debt. But did he retreat to burrow back under the bedsheets? Did he shout at her? Did he seek to undermine her every move? No, he did not. He faced the morning staunchly, bravely. Like a true soldier. A soldier of the city. And recently, a soldier of the suburbs. Just because he hadn't fought in the military didn't mean he couldn't feel powerful and manly.

Holding the bagel in his palm and slicing through, Harold carved a deep incision across his heart line. He stared, surprised, at the bright color of his blood, admired it for several seconds, and stuck his hand under the faucet, watching the pinkish stream of water flowing down the drain. "Damnit to hell," he said aloud, and wrapped a dishtowel around his hand, tying it with his teeth. Blood seeped through the towel.

"Ceremony! What's the point of it when you end up bleeding to death?"

He pushed down the lever and stood watching while the bagel, trapped in the element, began to smoke. He vaguely remembered he'd read about special toasters wide enough for bagels. He'd ask Betty about it. He reached into the toaster with the knife, fished out pieces of burnt bagel, and tossed the remains onto the counter. He went to the front door, knife in hand. As usual, the paper was curled up at the bottom step. He'd called the *Examiner* office several times to try to right the wrong but all he could reach was a computerized voice demanding he punch in a series of numbers. He couldn't take it, so he hung up. He'd write to them this afternoon and threaten them to use better aim or he'd cancel his subscription.

Harold gingerly stepped a bare foot onto the cold concrete steps, then the next, the soles of his feet instantly numb. Alex chose this exact moment to press his big paws onto the front door, whining to get outside to be with Harold, thinking it was time for his walk. As he did so, the door slammed shut and Harold was locked out.

Next door, church bells were pealing "Peace, I Ask of Thee, O River." Harold loved that melody. It soothed him. He would have to tell Betty to play that at his funeral. Whoever died must be important to have so many cars lined up so early in the morning. The obituaries would tell him who it was although he planned not to look because it would depress him. Maybe he could call Betty from the church phone just inside the side door. He tiptoed gingerly over the gravel road into the church parking lot. He could barely feel his feet, but he knew his body hair was standing at attention.

As cars eased into the church parking lot, their smooth entry was impeded by Harold. Dead center in the road, in full view, Harold was trying to appear composed: barechested, barelegged, barefaced, holding a bread knife, a dishtowel wrapped around one hand, with nothing on but the bright red boxer shorts Betty gave him for Father's Day. Every June, for the five years they'd been married, his wife wrapped beautiful packages with perky wire ribbon and glossy paper and presented them to him with a hopeful smile.

He just couldn't go into the church now, not with all those people paying their respects to a dead person. Locked out in the bitter winter chill, Harold ran back home and rang the doorbell several times before he remembered Betty was usually in the shower after breakfast. He was shaking in bodily places he forgot he had. He tiptoed to the garage door and tried to turn the doorknob. Cars slowed and drivers turned to stare.

In the bathroom, Betty was toweling dry, turning from one side to another admiringly, studying her reflection in the mirror and the tiny abdominal swelling that she was waiting until just the right moment to announce.

Tonight, she'd fix his favorite meal: meatloaf and mashed potatoes. Betty heard a dull popping sound from the kitchen and smelled sulfur and carbon. Overcooked eggs and burnt bagel.

"Harold!" she called. "Is that you?" No answer. "Harold?! Answer me, please!! Sweetheart?" Silence. She heard pounding on windows. Something was dreadfully wrong. She thought of that television commercial advertising 911. *Lives are often lost if you wait. Just pick up the phone and dial.* Not one to face terror alone, she threw on her robe, ran to the phone and called. 9-1-1. She was hyperventilating, her fingers shaking as she punched the buttons. She was scarcely able to stutter out their address. She felt faint.

Harold circled the house, pounding on every window. A gust of wind blew his thinning hair, sending a chill through him. He remembered the bathroom window which he usually left unlocked for fresh air. He could reach it on the side of the house next to the garage.

All he would have to do is get a couple of logs from the woodpile and stand on them. As he moved a few logs to the base of the bathroom window, loose bits of bark scraped off and stuck in the open slit in his hand. The dishtowel came loose and blood dripped down his thigh.

He noticed a silver Lexus circling the block. A line of cars slowed down behind the Lexus, faces pressed against closed windows. Harold piled the logs on the ground at the base of the bathroom window. He slid the bread knife under the sill and maneuvered it upwards, raising the window. In the distance, he heard a siren. As he lifted first one knee and then the other through the frame, he caught his shorts on the latch of the storm window, heard a rip, felt a cold breeze and crawled the rest of the way in. Just as he startled to see his reflection in the mirror, he saw a flashing red light in the periphery of his own image. He studied it for a few seconds, squinting, and then opened his eyes wide.

He definitely needed a new eyeglass prescription. Was he a good candidate for lasik surgery? Was he too old? Did he have too much astigmatism? He'd have to talk to his ophthalmologist. The front door bell was ringing. Betty was screaming softly, "Help! Help!"

Alex bounded toward Harold, half growling, face dripping with freshly-drunk toilet water. Harold greeted Alex with a reassuring "It's just me, Alex, It's Daddy!"

Alex licked his face with a long wet tongue, happy, oh so happy to see him again. Harold shivered in the sudden warmth of the steamy bathroom. He glanced again into the mirror, this time observing that he was wearing only his undershirt and the elastic to his boxer shorts, with a few strands of cloth attached. Most of his body was streaked with blood. He reached around to release his shorts from the latch, trying to gather the shreds of red fabric together. Harold was fully exposed.

He patted Alex on the head and shoved him back out of the way, gesticulating with the knife. "I'm going to change my ways, Alex. No more breakfast over the sink.

No more burnt bagels. From now on, it's Betty and me, sitting up at the table across from each other, reading the paper like an old married couple. Like Betty wants, not like a coupla nuts…" Harold said, as two burly cops with guns drawn burst into the cozy bathroom, one of them tripping over Alex.

Betty, shrinking behind the officers, was gasping for breath and hiccupping. She recognized Harold's voice just before he stood to raise his arms in protest, waving the knife over his head. "Officer, don't shoot!" she cried. "It's Harold!"

Too late. Alex caused the officer's gun to discharge, the bullet blasting from its chamber, up into the shower rod, which fell on Harold's head and knocked hm back against the floor, smack against the cold porcelain, back into the land of cold, cold dreams, the land where he used to live, before he met Betty, who brought him to the suburbs and to lovely Alex the Airedale who adored him, and to cops who tried to bring order to the town's citizens and protect them from terrible chaos.

Summoning the combined power of females through the ages, and following in the tradition of women at arms whose men are in danger, Betty ruthlessly shoved the officer aside and collapsed into a weeping heap across Harold's crumpled body.

"Harold," she sobbed. "Oh, Harold, I was going to surprise you tonight. We're expecting our first child."

Harold opened an eye and lifted one bloody hand to try to reach her head. "I'm so glad, Betty, darling. Little Harold." His voice was weak, as if calling to her from a distant place.

"Yes, sweetheart," Betty raised her head to look directly into Harold's spinning eyes, "or maybe a little Betty," wept Betty. "No more personal shopping."

Harold lay pale and limp. Behind his eyelids, he was transforming the Lichtenstein poster. The woman's lips were smiling in pure joy. "I remembered. I remembered," he muttered.

Harold never gave up. He still gripped the knife handle like a true warrior, finally home after a long battle spent seeking his rightful place in the world. Alex clambered over the feet of the police officers to delicately sniff Harold's naked body for identification, lay down on the cold tile floor, nuzzled his wet nose into Harold's warm armpit and whined.

Catch and Kill

I admit it was my idea. "I'd love to keep a few, enough for dinner anyway. Bring your stringer," I told Rudy.

Fourth of July weekend, when our lake place was packed full of children, grandchildren, and cousins, it was time. Our son, Rudy, is a catch and release guy. He has every conceivable type of plastic lure: worms, crayfish, squids, and leeches. He also uses real worms from Big Mike's which he stores in my refrigerator. If you didn't recognize the telltale blue Styrofoam, you might mistake it for vegetable dip. By letting him keep the container in my refrigerator, I am an accessory.

This has a history. Once, years ago, he and I decided to clean and gut an especially large fish.

"You said you'd do it!" I complained as we went behind the woodpile to do the deed.

"Heck, no! You said you would do it. That was the deal."

"No way. You do it."

"Absolutely not. We had an agreement."

"Well, okay, you kill it and I'll finish."

We were a regular comedy team.

We got a flat board. We found a knife. First he tried, then I tried sawing its head off. It flapped its large tail. Its

mouth opened and closed. My hands trembled. I was in tears. Rudy was angry. He grabbed the knife. The sound of the knife slicing through skin was sharp and grating. By the time he was done, there were blood and bones everywhere and just a couple of mouthfuls of fish to eat. Since then, it's reel 'em in and throw 'em back.

Right off the dock Rudy catches three pounders. At least that's what they look like to me. What do I know? I just dodge the lines. Usually there's a kid or two with a bamboo pole, another with a rod and reel, and Rudy, supervising. He acknowledges every fish caught, big and small, as a lakeside sacrament. Sometimes a photo is taken.

After Rudy or a child pulls in a fish, Rudy names the type and size, unhooks its tortured mouth; his glossy black lab retriever Momo, standing by, jumps up and licks it; everyone laughs at the dog; and Rudy flips the fish back in the water. The feistier ones or the sharp-toothed northerns who have slipped out of his hand slither back off the dock into the lake with an assist from the edge of someone's foot.

I've caught a fish or two in my lifetime. When I was five my great Uncle Reuben took me out in his little wooden boat and showed me how to string a worm. Something about Reuben — gentle voice with a thick Yiddish accent, ruddy cheeks, an old dirty cap, and his bright blue eyes shining at me from just under the brim —– of course, I couldn't disappoint him. We caught sunny after sunny, their golden bodies glimmering in the late afternoon sun. I don't remember feeling anything but loved, and the fat, pink worm as Uncle Reuben eased its body around the sharp hook. It took technique. It took steady fingers. It took delicate artistry and concentration. I've not threaded a worm since.

Then there was the time I caught a perch shore fishing in Venice, California. When my girlfriend's husband Gene, split open the belly of my prize to gut it, she was full of fry. Rows of fry, fifteen or so little fish, all perfect - perfect little eyes, perfect little noses, perfect little fins, all unborn, like little, silvery soldiers, lined up facing the same direction, ready to hatch. Instead, I executed them in one cast. That was it for me.

I could tell you more, like the time our family went deep sea fishing in Acapulco and my sister caught a sailfish. Our Mexican captain spread it over the prow of the boat for us to admire. It gave meaning to the word awesome. He smiled as he opened its deep violet, accordion sail, shining iridescent in the sun. Within minutes, the fish lay limp, its pride paled to dull brown.

I'm fine with just watching this dock activity, except when fish gasp for air while Rudy uses a pliars to remove the hook. Or when they flop around on the dock, struggling blind to find water, where they can wriggle and dive through the private darkness of lake weeds. Once the fish return to the lake, I utter a secret prayer to the lake gods : *Please take care of all your returnees. Please help them breathe. Please let them have a normal life.* I picture hundreds of them swimming around with ragged mouths and little angel halos magically suspended over their heads.

But I've been known to be greedy, like this time when I decided it was overdue to keep a few fish to eat. Our lake is small. There's no public access, no motors allowed. It's filled with thousands of northern, bass, sunnies, perch, and bluegills. Most of the guys in nondescript hats rowing silently by in Alumacrafts will say we need to slim down crowded conditions underwater. It's our responsibility. A duty to serve.

Out of nine residents on our lake maybe only Babs and her boys keep fish for food. More than once she has offered to clean my fish.

As I was saying, this Fourth of July I had a houseful — seven kids and six adults. They were bringing in fish by the dozen and tossing them back. Rudy knew my mind. Babs would be ready.

So when Rudy's older son, Jaguar, reeled in an impressive small mouth bass, Rudy said, "Get in the boat. Now!" He has a way about him. You love him and you resent him at the same time. He barks orders like a drill sergeant, but he's my son and I can't bring him up again. I tried once and anyone else might have done a better job.

I took my place at the bow, still wet from my last swim, towel wrapped around my waist. Behind us was the single bass on the end of a stringer, rocking and rolling in the small wake of the boat. His gills were bright yellow, the color of the stringer that served as guillotine and noose. He was the size of a small cat. Three of the boys, with Jag in the middle looking proud, took up the center seat. Rudy rowed down to the end of the lake to Babs' place.

Momo swam after us, trying to jump in the bow. He takes his jobs seriously: chief fish-licker and masthead. He tried to bite the twirling fish. Rudy discouraged him with his oar. He tried to climb in. I pushed him away. Reluctantly, he bounded back to shore and followed us along the shoreline until we got to Babs' cabin. He's in the water so much his coat shines like black enamel. When he's not in the water patrolling back and forth for fish, he's on the dock or in the boat.

"Babs!" I shouted. I untied the stringer from the boat and headed up the long wooden staircase. There she stood at the top, waiting, as if she were expecting us. "Still wanna do the job?" I held up the fish.

"Looks like you got yourself a good one," she said.

"Yup. Remember Jag? He's the fisherman. Remember Babs, Jag?" They nodded at each other. Jag squeezed ahead of me. He held up the fish and said, "Yah, I caught it with a plastic worm."

"C'mon out back," she said, a minister officiating at an important religious rite. Jag's little brother, Tran, their first cousin, Marv, Rudy and I followed her around back of her one-room cabin, the one without electricity, hot water or

I HEARD A FISH CRY and OTHER STORIES

plumbing. Behind her cabin, by the outhouse, was a fish-cleaning station complete with a fish fillet knife, long hose, and schpritzer for rinsing off the fish.

She picked up her knife. "Before you do that, can ya weigh it?" Rudy asked.

"Oh sure, be right back," Babs said, disappeared into her house and returned with a little weighing gizmo the size of a cell phone charger. It had a hook on the end of it and a little moveable gauge. She stabbed the fish's mouth with the hook several times, puncturing it all around, some perforations stretching into circular holes, until she found a spot under the lip that wouldn't rip and was thick enough to hold. "Two and a half pounds," she said, lifting it up. She whipped a tape measure out of thin air, transmogrifying from minister to magician, "18 ½ inches long."

"The size of a newborn baby," I whispered. The fish was still alive. Its eyes were slate. Unreadable. Eternal. Its accordion gills were pleated bright red, flaring open and shut. Its long underside was pale lemon edged by a deep green body.

Babs began her sermon, intended to soothe. "Your fish is feeling pretty numb by now. It was on a stringer off the side of the boat. It's been out of the water a good while so it won't feel much." Her face carries a plump sweetness, like a ripe strawberry. She brought out the knife. A glint of sunlight struck its edge.

The boys' noses met the edge of the fish station, a north country's baptismal font. Rudy stood guard behind them, his hands on Tran's shoulders.

I remember Rudy, age four, covering his own genitals at his little brother's circumcision. If he could have melted into the walls, he would have.

The boys were starting to ask questions. My ears were buzzing. I heard nothing but my own thoughts. How could I have done this? They were so innocent. I tiptoed backwards and turned toward the boat landing. I hurried down the steps to the boat. It was scorching hot. If I got in the boat, I'd scald my legs.

I thought back to other times Babs came in handy. One weekend last summer, she spotted some guys in a boat with a motor on our lake. Before I could get down to my dock to talk to them, she was on my lawn, shouting - gently of course, but with volume.

No one does that around here. No one ever trespasses. It's very private.

"Fellas. Hey, fellas!" Babs put the full strength of her ample girth behind her voice. "There's an ordinance on the lake thatcha can't be on the water with a motor! So wherever you came from, you'd better g'wan back now. Otherwise, I'll have to call the sheriff. 'Preciate it."

As she was shouting, I remembered the pile of fish guts I'd seen on the road driving in. I hustled over to her and under my breath, said, "Hey, while you're at it, wouldja ask them if they're the ones who left the pile of fish guts down the road? We've got turkey vultures circling overhead."

"Hey, guys, next time, also make sure when you clean your fish ya bury it someplace deep and out of the way? Sure do 'preciate it!"

I didn't hear a reply, but knew they were on their way back to wherever they came from. Next day the fish guts were gone, and the vultures on another journey. Yup. She's a good neighbor to have around.

So, when it came to taking her up on her offer to clean our fish, I took the bait. Hook, line, and sinker. I also convinced my reluctant son.

I hovered around the boat awhile and climbed back up the long flight to the sacrificial altar. All four sets of once-virginal eyes were fixed on the aftermath. Babs handed Rudy a small baggie with cut up fillets. A very large head still attached to the guts and bowels of the bass went into another. I took it.

"Thanks a lot, Babs," I said when her eyes met mine. "Sorry, I just couldn't watch." I was choking on my words.

Babs looked at me, misty-eyed. "When we kill our hunt, we thank the gods for the sacrifice. We thank the gods for our good hunt. We thank the gods for food."

To myself I said, *It's so much easier to go to the grocery store.*

Down we clambered toward the boat. On the way, I picked up a fallen lawn ornament, a penguin, hollow and plastic. Babs stood once again at the top of the stairs. I tried to right the penguin, but it kept tipping over. I climbed up the hill to get a log from her pile to level the bird. I felt virtuous being able to help her in some way.

"That penguin came from your property, from the first owner. There's one just like it at the opposite end of the lake. They keep watch, " she said.

Weird, I thought. *This isn't exactly Antarctica. What's wrong with a bald eagle?*

"Penguins symbolize agility, order and the ability to move through various dimensions of life."

"Really? Hmm. I'll work on that."

I waved, thanked her again, as Rudy whipped off my towel from my waist and gave it to his children to sit on.

"What am I supposed to sit on?"

Rudy handed me his shirt, an afterthought, but a generous and fitting gesture.

Off we rowed. All were silent on the row back home. As soon as our dock came into view, Jag spoke through the stupefied air.

"I never knew they could do that," he said to no one in particular.

"Do what?" I asked.

"Wag their tails after they're cut."

We got out of the boat. "Come with me to bury the guts," I said to Jag. He followed me. I got a shovel. The deer flies were bad. I found a spot in the sun by the rose bush. I dug hard, cutting the sharp spade into the earth, slicing through roots, digging and digging. The hole had to be big enough to keep away bears and vultures who feel no remorse, but smell a carcass for miles. No hole seemed deep enough to hide the remains of the trophy fish. His head was half the size of Jag's.

Jag started to wail and ran away. "Come back here!" I yelled. "This is your fish. You help me bury it!"

"But the deer flies are biting me!"

"Right, they're biting me too! Now get back here and help!"

There was nothing for him to do but bear witness. I had the shovel and he had nothing but my words. He came back and stood by, stamping the ground and whining, as I poured the fish remains from the baggie into the hole. The fish slid in, spiraling, mouth up, eyes round and black. "Now help me cover it up!"

"With what?" he wailed.

"Our hands!"

I leaned over in my wet bathing suit and brought the shoveled dirt over the hole. Flies drew blood from my back. We couldn't keep them away. Jag kept smacking at his legs, half-heartedly kicking a small bit of earth over the hole with the toe of his sandal. I was on my knees, scratching and pulling at the soil.

"C'mon, Jag. You were so proud of your fish. Now let's finish the job!" I wanted him to know how precious the life of the fish was. I wanted him to understand what happens when you kill something. I wanted him to suffer the way I was suffering. I wanted him to feel my grief and moisten the mound, the small graveyard by my rosebush, with his tears.

Condor's Raw Side

He hopped out of his battered truck and propelled himself forward in bobbing quail-like bursts. The glare of the Superamerica sign beamed off his bald head. He wore stiff new jeans, cuffs rolled up. He pressed his lips together, rolled his forehead into a frown. A large black Newfoundland dog barked and paced across the open flatbed behind the cab, rocking the truck back and forth. The dog's left side was totally shaved, his hindquarters raw as roadkill. The dog weighed a hundred and fifty pounds, easy.

"Stay, Condor," he commanded, and turned toward me where I stood watching at the gas station door. I opened the door for both of us and headed toward the ATM. I swiped my plastic card through the magic slot while Condor's Master studied the selection of fast food behind me. I used to believe a tiny square man lived in the ATM machine, surviving off a diet of paper. He had a photographic memory of every bank balance and a tiny typewriter where he wrote your receipt. I couldn't bring myself to shove my card into the slot, forcing just one more burden on this besieged little man. But I stopped believing in him and now I believe in the magic of instant money.

"Nice pooch. Looks like he just had surgery. How's he

doin'?" I said, over my shoulder, as I punched in my password. Nothing to it after you do it a few times.

"Well, actually, he's not too great. He's out of the loop." I turned to face him, in the middle of my transaction, showing off.

"What loop?" I said. He came over and stood next to me, watching as I punched in *$100.00, withdrawal, checking, receipt required.*

"At the park. There's a little place where I bring him twice a day to run around with his dozen or so buddies. There's a Wolfhound-Shepherd mix, a Malamute-Husky, a Rottweiler, a Cockapoodle, a Chow, a Golden Lab, a Golden Retriever and about five smaller ones that try to keep up. They've all been tight until lately. Condor's stigmatized because of his illness. The Golden Lab who used to be his best friend, ignores him and plays with the pack. Condor can't keep up with them anymore."

"How old is Condor?"

"Almost five."

"Aw, he'll get his spunk back," I said.

"It's taken a lot out of him. I don't know if he'll ever be the same." His lower lip quivered and he turned away from me to pluck a bag of Cheetos off the shelf. I put my forty dollars away into my purse and went to the counter where he stood with his choices: a plastic gallon of Diet Pepsi, loaf of Wonder bread, Cheetos, can of tuna fish, and spray rug cleaner. I knew there was more to his story and somehow felt obliged to listen.

The clerk rang his order. She chewed gum in rhythm to "Jingle Bell Rock."

From her left ear dangled a shiny green globe and off her right, a red. A lit up reindeer was pinned to her red jacket.

She shoved his items into a thin paper sack and looked past him. "Fifteen fifty-six!" she said as he handed her a twenty.

"The worst part is," he went on, "he won't eat. After his chemo treatments, he gets really sick and upchucks all over the house. I've tried everything. I've given him enriched vitamin/mineral supplements, beans, brown rice, lentils, lean beef, tofu, cottage cheese. The vitamins cost sixty-five dollars for twenty. His vomit's radioactive. I wear rubber gloves."

"Next!" the cashier shouted, slapping his change on the counter. The man behind him, wearing a bright ski hat and neon pink jacket, shifted his weight from one leg to another like he was ready to kill a double black diamond slope in Aspen. Condor's Master stood firmly in place. The skier nudged me in the back. I looked back at him and he furrowed his brow, twitched the corners of his mouth and shook his head. The cashier winked at him.

"That'll be twenty-three dollars and fifty-five cents for the supreme gas, sir. Merry Christmas."

The man behind me reached over me to hand her some money. She punched open the register. Condor's Master slid his package off the counter with slow deliberation and turned toward the door. "It's not supposed to be like this, such a sick dog, so sick, my best friend, especially during the holidays," he said half to me, half over his shoulder to the skier who followed him.

"Look, asshole, no one wants to hear about you and your fuckin' dog, get it? You're holdin' up the line!" He shoved Condor's Master through the exit door. I ran after Condor's Master.

I held his package while he opened the back gate to the truck. Out sprang Condor, soaring into the air with all the power of a thunderbird. His feathery flanks took wing. His jaw opened. His three good legs and one gimpy one stretched across to their target. His target was opening the door to his forest green Jaguar.

Down came Condor, down on the skier's back.

"Oomph!" said the skier, his face hitting first his door and then the oily snow.

He moaned and muttered into the mute ground, turning his face from side to side, trying to get up. Dirty snow crystals clung to his battered face.

Condor's front paws fastened his prey to the ground.

"Here, Condor! Let's go home now!" his Master commanded. A thin trickle of blood crawled toward the gas pump. Mighty Condor wagged his tail, jumped off the skier and ran in a circle, smiling and barking.

"Up, boy," Condor's Master patted the rear gate for Condor to jump up. Condor stuck his nose in the bag of Cheetos spread in the snow. Condor gobbled down a mouthful, swallowed half the loaf of Wonder bread, gave a huge leap and settled his bulk inside, raw side out. Condor's Master closed the rear gate and bobbed over to the skier to lift him up from under the armpits.

"Condor knows everything that happens to me. I don't have to tell him. I know you didn't mean what you said. Have a happy holiday season, sir."

Chunks of ice, oil and debris stuck to the skier's bleeding forehead and cheeks.

"Sure, buddy," he said, lowering himself into his Jaguar. Two dark paw prints marked the back of his shiny pink jacket. He held his soiled hat in his hand.

Condor's Master bobbed back to his truck. He banged the back window to greet Condor and swung into the front seat. I handed him what was left of his groceries.

"Condor looks happy now! Have a great holiday!" I said.

The Case of The Disappearing Dogs

It was one of those mysteries where you think you know the answer but it's too awful so you don't want to admit it. It would ruin your life if it were true. Maybe forever. Well, maybe that's an exaggeration. At least it would ruin your outlook for a very long time. Seriously alter your attitude, for which you would need years of therapy.

None of us is perfect. My grammar is excellent. Hence, subject verb agreement of the subject none as in not one person, singular, with the verb is, also singular. No one is perfect. My grammar may be excellent, but it's not perfect. Sometimes I get confused about things like she said to whoever would listen as opposed to she said to whomever would listen. When other people continually use the wrong grammar, it's a constant battle to remember the right way. Me and George wanna go home. I mean really. Must we accept this kind of verbal corruption?

In any case, this story is not about grammar, but it is about acceptance of others' weaknesses, which can be difficult. I hope you will listen to this story, because it is a tragedy and tragedies can teach us. Especially Greek tragedies which this isn't. But it's a good one anyway. And it may teach you something.

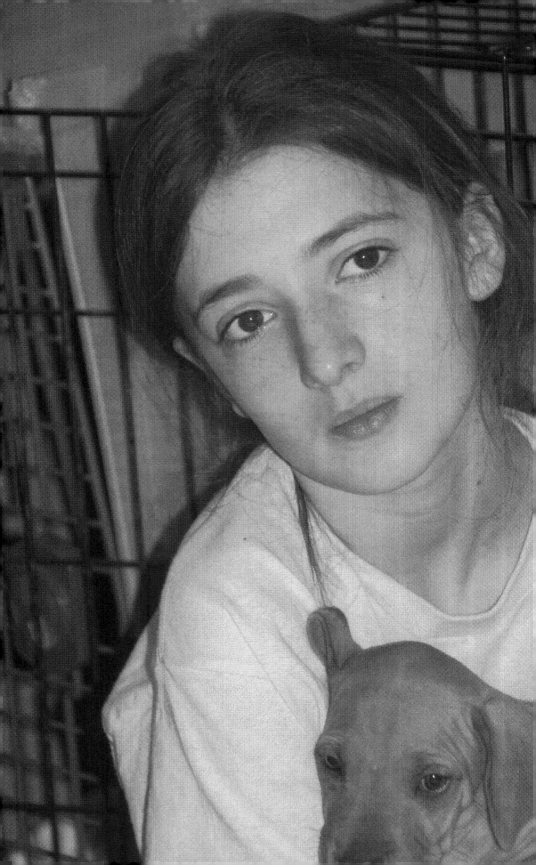

My mother had a difficult childhood. Hence, she was a difficult mother. I mean it's important to say that at the beginning—that being the root cause of the story. Or at least one of the root causes. My mother's mother was crazy—schizophrenic. My mother was at the mercy of her father who was middle-aged and didn't have the slightest notion of how to bring her up so he discharged her to the care of boarding schools where she learned elocution and manners and tried to be a good girl, trusting that those were the most important things one could learn from an adult.

We had a series of dogs in our home. A series of disappearing dogs. First there was Meg the cocker spaniel with the caramel velvet coat and the beautiful brown eyes. I was too little to wonder about her disappearance but I know she existed and there's a photo of me squatting down, holding her collar, looking completely in love, underpants sagging down into the grass, tongue hanging out between missing front teeth.

Next, there was Krisky, a fox terrier, full of spunk and tricks. I have no idea what happened to her. Next came Buffin. He was the dog I remember loving a lot. I had lots of pet names for him, Mr. Bufforfington being the best one. A very large and cruel German Shepherd named Koenig came into our yard before anyone could stop him and tore him to bits. He was repaired and as soon as he was released from the hospital, Koenig returned and vanquished little Buffin again. I don't think I saw Buffin after that. I'd like to believe I was deliberately spared anguish, but I think Buffin's brave spirit could have been like a phoenix, despite Koenig. Out of three dogs, he was the only one who had even close to a natural death. I couldn't properly grieve him because Buffin simply disappeared the way Meg and Krisky had. It never occurred to me to pursue the mystery of dog disappearance because if I did, the answer was always the same, "I don't know, dear, what happened. _____ (fill in the blank with the name of the dog) must have disappeared." It's hard to cry over someone when you are led to believe s/he never existed in the first place.

Charlie Sam was my last dog and the only one truly mine. For my sixteenth birthday, my sister and her husband gave me this wonderful dog who was mostly beagle. I had him three days. During those three days, I kept him in bed with me and loved his gentle self as much as I could since I sensed his days would be numbered. But, I had to go to school during the day and leave Charlie Sam in the care of the mother I mentioned. She kept him in the garage where it was dark and cold and his lonely barking fell on deaf ears. I knew he cried all day because his voice was hoarse when I opened the door and he jumped all over me and carried on like he'd been in jail all day, which he had.

The first two days went all right. I hurried home and rescued him from a mysterious disappearance. On the third day, I brought home reinforcements —my pal, Johni. On the way home, I said to her, "I'm afraid Charlie will be gone."

"What do you mean, gone?"

"Disappeared. All our dogs have disappeared. I think my mother does it."

"Does what?"

"Makes them disappear."

"No, she wouldn't do that. Who would do that?"

"My mother."

Well, you can guess what happened. I pulled open the garage door and Charlie was gone. I called to him and called to him and ran in the house, crying. My friend Johni stood in the driveway, her mouth dropped open. She tried to comfort me, but I was old enough to understand that there was something terribly wrong with this picture.

Skipping ahead to my life as an adult, you can fill in some details. Yes, I needed therapy. And, yes, I had a houseful of dogs as soon as I had a house to put them in, and yes, I loved them and cared for them, and watched over them. Every last one. And there were many, many dogs. First there was Izzy, a beautiful curly-haired mixed breed who ran in the street and was run over. Next came our first Bearded Collie, Samoset, who lived to age 12. We got him a wife, Cinnamon, and they had six puppies —Angus, Oatmeal, Gizmo, Gus, Shiksa, and Blue. Then came Shadrach, our next Bearded Collie, his wife Mishach, their three litters— Adeline, Abigail and Abner; Bentley and Boudreau; Calliope and Cedars. I bred dogs to make sure there were enough for me at all times.

Significant to this story is that my mother actually wanted to name our last sire, Shadrach. We thought seriously of Stravinsky, but took the biblical route. It was clear Mother needed redemption, and after all, the story of Daniel walking around in a pit of fire is enough to inspire the hardest of hearts.

My therapist, Big Eyes, asked me about my mother. I tried to explain, but the subject somehow boiled down to disappearing dogs. She said, "Let's get to the bottom of this. Invite her in."

After much protestation, I called my mother in. I told her I'd been depressed. She felt some sympathy for that and agreed to come in, although it was clear she didn't like the idea one bit. I explained to her that it wouldn't be too scary and that I loved her no matter what and that I forgave her for everything.

I brought her to the therapy scene. I confronted her. "What happened to all the dogs we had?"

"What dogs?" (Here we go again, I thought).

"All the dogs—Meg. Krisky. Buffin. Charlie Sam."

"Well, Koenig took after Buffin and he was never the same," Mother was triumphant. She thought that was going to be the end of the discussion.

"So what did you do with him?"

"I took him to the animal refuge and had him put to sleep." I could scarcely believe my ears. Not only was she acknowledging that there had been a Buffin, but she admitted that she had a hand in his demise. Now I was triumphant.

"And what about Charlie Sam?"

"You mean that dog your sister's ex-husband gave you?"

"Yes."

"He never should have done that. I couldn't take care of him. It was more than I could handle."

"Then why didn't you ask me to do that?"

"I don't know, dear, I suppose I didn't like the fact that he brought him over without permission."

"So because you were mad at him, you killed the dog?"

"I didn't kill him." Triumph again.

"What did you do?"

"I don't remember, dear."

"Try to remember."

"I suppose I bought him to the humane society."

"How did you get him there?"

"I suppose I drove him."

"So you drove Charlie Sam to the humane society and left him there?"

"Yes, I must have."

"You realize they probably killed him."

"Perhaps."

"Why didn't you tell me?"

"Because I was ashamed."

"Ashamed?"

"Yes."

I studied Mother's face for a whiff of emotion. Not finding any, I thanked her for her admission and we concluded our session. It had certainly been enough for me.

I talked to my mother on the phone shortly thereafter and thanked her again, telling her I was sorry she had felt ashamed and that I appreciated her honesty.

"Ashamed?" she said, shocked. "Ashamed for what? I never said I was ashamed for anything dear. Whatever are you talking about?"

As I said, no one and nothing is perfect. Not memory. Not personality. Not life. Some things are a mystery. Some things are not.

Recovery

Bodybuilding consumed Lydia. Her muscles were boulders, pumped with steroids. Every tendon strained its sheath. When she lost the last competition, she turned her glossy back, stepped out of her G-string and bikini top—a howling, naked feral animal—and crept to the granite rock to reclaim her natural power.

Meanwhile, her family, folded into deck chairs, stared into the ocean and waited, pretending not to notice. Sanders, her husband, knew the signs. He observed her climbing out of sight. He read the *Atlantic* and, when he was done with that, the *New York Times* Sunday edition and the *Economist*. Her mother glared into the setting sun, eyes fixed. Out of her peripheral vision, beyond the grassy plain, up into the hillside, to the spot where she sat on the granite rock, she watched. Her younger brothers believed she should get a woman's job but stayed for the show.

Lydia sat naked for three days straight. She knew there were coyotes. Cougars. She felt their kinship. She also knew that Sanders would be there when the drugs and defeat drained from her softening body, when she crept back through the field of tall grass that waved in the sun between the hills.

Lydia approached them slowly, the four of them: Sanders, her mother, her two brothers. Closer she came, rising up out of the numbness named loss, the glow of poses and lights and oils she used to slick her body into a sheen that, by now, had faded away.

Down toward them, one step at a time.

Pulling Calves:
HERMOSA, SOUTH DAKOTA

The corral is bathed in moonlight. It's cold enough for many layers of wool and heavy mittens. We're closing in on the moment I imagined—the birthing of a calf. To Jeanne, it's routine; to me, it's a new miracle. I'm her city friend—raw, but ready. She has invited me into her world and I'm trying, but failing, to suppress my enthusiasm. In hushed tones, we crunch across the ice to aim a flashlight under the tails of snorting, pregnant heifers. How long the rancher waits for the cow to give birth before she's assisted is a matter of time, based on experience and guesswork.

"Not an exact science," Jeanne says, "but it works...usually." I've been nagging her since dinner to "check on things." Reluctantly, she agrees. My feet itch from the hay inside my socks and my boots have lost traction from manure clotted on the soles. Our frequent trips back and forth break me in.

This time, we're lucky. A big white cow leans against the fence, quietly munching grass with two hooves sticking conspicuously out her rear end. Jeanne gives me a wry smile and says, "You have good instincts!" She coaxes the heifer into the barn, at first carefully, and then when that doesn't work, less carefully (mostly running around in circles after her).

In the stall, we watch the cow's weak and irregular contractions, standing out of her way. I am busy dreaming up names, reciting them aloud. The cow is Miranda, and the calf will be Carmen or Jesse (after the singer and politician). As I sit musing on a bale of hay, I turn to see Jeanne's arm thrust well up Miranda's uterus.

"Checking on the size of the calf's head," she tells me.

"With those hands, you could make more money picking locks," I say.

"Probably a Charolais. Just can't keep the neighbor's bull out. Huge head. This heifer's not big enough. Could be trouble."

It's after midnight.

We go back for more clothes and Jeanne's father. We're barely able to move in two pairs of pants, four shirts, a hat and several blankets. On the other hand, James, her eighty year old father, maneuvers easily in a pair of jeans and thin jacket, naked back exposed to subzero weather. Jeanne has tried to toss a rope over the cow's head but she is tired and the rope falls limp to the barn floor. Without comment, James tosses it once just behind Miranda's head. The cow is immediately encircled by a loop whose end he tethers to a post with several knots to prevent the cow's thrashing.

With a leather strap and a metal bar to wrap around the cow's hips, chains and a grappling hook, the whole procedure is like pulling a car out of a ditch in Minnesota. This will be the equivalent of a forceps birth. Jeanne rinses the chains in warm water before she wraps them around the calf's hooves now sticking out to the knees. To pull the calf out by chains leaving hooves intact calls for just the right amount of pressure, leverage and empathy. A calf crippled by too much pulling and wrong timing will not survive. It's a cooperative labor calling for the right rhythm between gears, or in this case, contractions.

Contractions ripple from behind her front legs back toward her tail with the force and plunge of a ship in a hurricane. Jeanne plants her feet, pulls backward, straining, trying not to tear her back muscles or the cow's cervix. She grits her teeth and uses her full weight until, with a slurp, the full front legs along with the calf's head emerge. Heartened, she continues to pull until the entire calf is freed.

"Get out of the way, child, in case she kicks," James says, almost inaudibly. "Yes, father; you, too." It's a call and response akin to "The Lord be with you...And also with you."

Miranda, suddenly aware of our presence, decides to let us take over her other chores as well and slides back to the barn floor with a grunt and a heavy thud. She seems to have lost interest in this birthing business.

"Sometimes," Jeanne tells me, "heifers aren't quite up to it. We can lose them and the calf. Sometimes, they're both healthy, but the cow's a lousy mother."

Jeanne loosens the rope around the cow's head and gives her room while we listen to each other's breathing. Within moments, a soaking wet, wobbly-headed, rather stupid looking baby bull has fully emerged—Jesse. Jeanne rubs him down with a towel to warm and stimulate him, a job Miranda should be doing with her tongue. I try to lift Jesse's heavy body, dropping his head downward so excess fluid drains out of his lungs. He is huge, heavier than he looks, and slippery. He curls back up into his folded-up fetal position. His breath is a rattle. He ought to stand and show his strength. I try again. James encourages me. I decide to change my career and become a veterinarian.

Jesse's white head is irresistibly soft and I want to embrace his beautiful warm body long into the night.

"Time to go," Jeanne says softly. "Miranda could charge us."

"No way. Check out those big brown eyes."

"Right. But, it's still her baby, not ours."

If we stay in the barn any longer, several things may happen. One, a skunk who has been peeking his head out from under the tools in the corner, may appear full-bodied. Two, Miranda's mothering will be further delayed. Three, we'll freeze solid.

Jeanne pulls the light chain in the barn and back we stumble across the wind-whipped prairie to our chilly beds. I'm full of joy and Jesse's dampness. My night is packed with dreams of my own children, the crowning, the cries. The next day I take an entire roll of film of Jesse, standing by himself in the corral. Miranda is not in sight.

Weeks later, after I've returned to the city, the snow has turned gray and I have not become a veterinarian, I receive a letter from Jeanne. I tear open the envelope, hungry for news of Jesse. Maybe she knew all along. But when she tells me, she cushions the news between other stories: "Spring's first meadowlark trills on the fence," she writes. "I'm sorry to tell you Jesse didn't make it. As Father and I drive across pasture, we're grateful the angle of the sun has shifted just enough to light up the dewy tufts of fur sticking up from newborn calves. Otherwise, we'd miss them lying curled up and hidden in the tall, waving buffalo grass."

Hansel And Gretel

Miriam and I are fast-walking around Big Lake. She, disciplined and virtuous,punches the air with clenched fists, checks her pulse. I, wavering and vagrant, talk to every dog, retie my shoelaces, study the sunset leaking across the lap of the lagoon.

When we arrive at St. Cloud, our neighborhood's most elegant street, I spy a vintage GMC van parked beside the curb.

A long extension cord slinks up the brick path to the os of a sedate stone mansion. The van is crudely painted, white panels tagged with battle cries about honor and courage. Hanging on one side is a large, hand-carved wooden shield painted blue with a yellow cross. Above that, hand-fashioned armaments: a jousting stick, brass fittings and ropes of chain. Across the front bumper stretches a big steel kangaroo bar.

"Imagine the clanging," I say.

"Yes," Miriam says, laughing. "Minnesota isn't exactly the outback."

"But it can be cruel to the overexposed," I say. "Check out that brass nozzle next to the door. What do you suppose it is?" I ask Miriam.

"A mezuzah," says Miriam, a spokesperson for Israel bonds in her spare time.

"I never have my camera when I need it," I say.

A man's square head appears between the jalousie slats of a small window in the side of a van. A black and white cat with black spots winds around his neck like a boa.

"Hello," the head says.

"Hello," we say back.

The cat meows.

The man peers out at us, blue eyes dilated wide and unblinking, neck rim of his t-shirt frayed and gray. Crudely carved amulets hang down between his hungry eyes.

"We're admiring your van," I say.

"This is my home," the van man says. "I live for the environment. I fight traffic.

I go the speed limit when no one else does. The shield you see is like Joan of Arc's. She was a crusader too. People tell me to do things just like they did to Joan. Some of them are evil. I got rolled once." The man pauses, lowers his head, waiting, confused.

Miriam cocks her head. I shift my weight.

"But your shield is the flag of Sweden, not France," I say, bent on accuracy, filling the awkward spot.

"Good eye!" he exclaims, raising his head. "My ancestors are Swedish. I modified the shield. I lived in this house but I moved to Wisconsin. Everything has a meaning. I suffered a tragedy."

"Oh," Miriam says, "I'm sorry." Miriam is courteous.

"Now I'm afraid to leave my van," Van Man says.

"What kind of tragedy?" I try to sound controlled like her, but my flat, two-dimensional tone creeps in, the one I keep handy when I sense my cover loosening.

"My cat, Gretel, burned to death. I couldn't get to her in time. When I found her, she was already fried. The boy cat here is Hansel. We're both in deep grief."

"Yes," Miriam repeats.

"How did it happen? A gas heater?" I ask.

Van Man nods. "What happened was this. Someone called me from the outside.

He wanted me to hurry, get dressed and come out. I left before I fully checked everything. I should never do that. We shouldn't be hasty. I'm not fixing any blame here, though. No blame. Gretel's gone is all."

"Yes," says Miriam. "No one's to blame."

The warrior in me struggles with that acceptance routine. Hell with that bullshit. He should've checked. Irresponsible SOB. Which version of Hansel and Gretel was he thinking of? And what's his role in the fairytale? Is he the evil witch? What's that I smell cooking in his van? Or is he the poor widowed parent, at the end of his rope, who carelessly loosed Hansel and Gretel at the edge of nowhere to find resources in the forest to bring home, shocked when Gretel didn't come home? In any case, he's guilty.

The peacemaker in me believes that Van Man is doing the best he can for the moment, that he has acknowledged the reality of Gretel's death, and that's all he can do. Hamlet said, "There is nothing good or bad, but thinking makes it so." (Hamlet, II,ii, 259).

I can't help remembering an old bluesy melody. "My baby's gone, gone, gone. . . waah, ah…" Van Man has the blues. They go in four stages: Love, Death, Wondering Why and Acceptance. Van Man hasn't transitioned out of the Death stage. Some of us don't ever escape.

"I was married once, about ten years ago. I wear the necklace she gave me right here." He taps a piece of petrified wood hanging between his famished eyes.

"I pay her tribute, but she doesn't have a collar on me anymore." He rubs his neck. "The other ones are from people I've met along the way who've gotten into my head." His slender fingers fondle the amulets. "My name's Victor. What's yours?"

I introduce myself, imagining his attenuated fingers tracing the outline of my ribs, smoothing my spine. Maybe I can help him get through Death and Wondering so we can move into Acceptance together.

An older man, grey hair, grey complexion, probably Victor's father, backs his Mercedes out of the driveway, stops briefly to scowl at us. I smile and say "Hello!" to the face behind the rolled-up window.

"He hates me, "Victor says.

His father drives away as I stand waving. Victor, Don Quixote casting at windmills, is linked to his father by a trailing umbilicus leading to the womb of his original home, the mansion. He is wasting his time trying to get his father's approval.

"I'd like to take some pictures of your van," I say. "Would that be all right, if I come back and take some pictures?"

"Oh, yes, that would be fine. I'll be here."

"Okay then, we'll see you," I say.

"Take good care, ladies," Victor says. Miriam and I fast-walk home a few blocks away. Miriam dismisses him as "certifiable." I am making plans.

As soon as Miriam leaves, I grab my camera. When I go back to the van, I hear sobbing and choking from inside. I can't bring myself to snap the shutter. I close up my camera, knock on the door. He opens it wide, stark naked, face covered in tear slime, gasping for breath.

"How goes the b-b-battle?" Victor asks, wiping his eyes with the back of his beautiful long arm.

"Battle?" I try to look into his eyes, not at his naked body. I am wowed. His eyes are the color of violet crocuses popping up out of earth. "Battle," I repeat, feeling stupid. Stupid, embarrassed, and guilty.

The warrior in me feels guilty for not fighting more battles of the world, berating myself for not doing more, talking a good game, living off the fat of the land, getting my pay check and spending it. The realist in me sees Victor driving around, stoned, afraid to get out of his van, trapped in an era those of us who survived want to forget, a by-product, like taconite tailings no one but suckers like me want to clean up. I won't revert to the sorry Seventies when I volunteered at prisons and marched for peace, when drugs nearly took me out.

On one hand, Victor, who still holds on to those good old peace and love values, might rekindle my flickering light, and I can spark his. On the other hand, curiosity killed his cat. Neither one of us has reached a state of full acceptance.

"C-Come in," Victor says, rolling his hand in a circle and bowing low. I lower my head and enter the van, which is stripped of all but the driver's seat. There are two electrical outlets overloaded with wires for a coffee pot, hot plate, tape deck and trouble light. Against the wall are a cot, a litter box, crates spilling over with soiled clothes and cans of Dinty Beef Stew. Hansel sprawls on his back on the cot, claws curled up. The walls are plastered with bumper stickers like "Save the Whales," "Save the Redwoods," "Jesus Saves." The air smells of jasmine incense, carnation aftershave, and ginger root. A dark glob of assorted vegetable mush is congealed to the sides of a porcelain pot on a hot plate. Victor gestures for me to sit in one of two aluminum frame folding chairs with frayed green and white webbing. Then he sits down facing me, our knees touching. Tiny hairs above the flat spots of my kneecaps electrify. I've never sat in a van with a naked man.

I try to hide my camera. I want to embrace his soul, not his van. Besides, I know Pro-Ex will never develop him in the buff. I play with the strap of my zipped-up camera bag and survey the landscape.

Under the jalousie window is a large poster of muscle-bound Daniel, from the Old Testament Book of Daniel, reclining amongst a cave full of ravenous lions. The poster says, "Contrary to conventional wisdom, stress is not a 20th century phenomenon." I chuckle into my lap before I dare to glance up at Victor. I am dazzled by his coffee mocha color, his feline grace, his raw, unfurled power. I want to frolic in the soft, golden hair that shines from his sinewy limbs like sunlit grass trailing across a prairie.

He reaches over my shoulder to click in Blood, Sweat and Tears on the tape deck. "What goes up, must come down, spinning wheels, all around." Wait, that was the seventies and this is a new century. What am I doing here? Is there something to learn, something I never quite got? His hollow eyes swallow me up. The hairs on my knees have collapsed and I am apple butter, all gooey and thin. He leans over to stare into my eyes. I like the fervor of his medieval sensitivity, but resist the glow of his skin.

He snorts with excitement and pulls out a Brown and Williamson roller and Zigzag papers. I'm dizzy from time warp. Just as I'm about to take a drag, readying to pass into an old world, I remember I've carved out a new life. I'm a "responsible" adult, worrying about stuff, getting to the job on time, pleasing others, striving to be satisfied with my existence, things when I was stoned, I dismissed. One whiff of that sweet seduction and I clear my throat.

"It's time to establish some guidelines, dear Victor," I begin. "Our mysteries don't mix. I cope in new ways." I stroke his arm the way I stroke the top of my dog's head. Nice Victor. Good boy, Victor. Hearing the delicious spark of his ignited Zigzags doesn't change the counterfeit of euphoria.

"It's good for what ails you. C'mon, it'll take the edge off," he says.

"Victor, burning to ash the energy I have left in me would be a big mistake. Little cats. Big lion. You can't change what was. I've come from more than one lifetime of cinders. What counts is forgiving yourself." A train passes over the tracks between his van and my home. Clackety, clackety. Our intersection is dangerous.

"About the poster," I say.

"Does it apply to you?" Victor tries to melt me down with his crocus eyes.

"That's a subject for another day. Gotta go, kiddo," I

say, standing up, forgetting the limits of the van, bumping my head.

"I'll light your cinders anytime. Just come on in whenever you see my van," he says, purring. He morphs from lion to Daniel and back to Victor. We're all players in this strange, schizophrenic hallucination.

"Before I go, I'd like to take your picture," I say. "Put some clothes on and stand in front of the willows." I wait outside while Victor finds just the right armor to suit the pose. He hops out, unhooks the jousting stick from the van and looks straight into the camera, smiling. I'm surprised at how at peace a photograph can make a person look.

Every holiday, when children return to families, Victor plugs in up the street. I return each time, establishing clear boundaries. He wears clothes. We stick to safe topics. He waxes eloquent about environmental pollution. We discuss saving oak trees and Indian burial grounds from highway engineers, research on frogs with three legs swimming crookedly upstream near a plastics factory, and polar bears in a land of diminishing ice.

We listen to *Jimi Hendrix Live at Woodstock*. I inhale the groove of Jimi's first ray of rising sun where I left off in 1969, but without the weed. Victor's a pothead, a repentant pet abuser, and maybe a shaman. He's also a good friend who offers me practice in just being. We're working toward the same end, doing our part to be who we are, to live to the ultimate, giving of ourselves until we're ready to become food for earth.

"Lions don't frighten me anymore. I like to just hang out, watching their tails flick back and forth, digging the rhythm," I tell him.

"My maiden in distress," he says.

"I'm no longer in distress," I say. "Forgiveness is everything. I put myself at the top of the list."

"Don't forget to amble along, notice the way the sun shines from behind the willows, their silhouettes painted against the sky," he says.

"I promise," I say.

I give him the photograph of himself, holding a jousting stick, long tendrils of willow draping down behind him. I'm grateful he was smiling.

In the spring, Victor changes form, becoming a solo crocus that pops up, seemingly at random, through spring-melted snow, and dropped his head back down into thinning ice.

It's a dark forest out there. A trail of bread crumbs is no guarantee.

Is That Your Deer?

It was a beautiful, warm, autumn afternoon, full of sunlight and laughter. I burst from my house, happy to greet the low angling sun overhead and crushed leaves underfoot. On the city sidewalk, a few yards ahead of me strode a ten-point buck, apparently unconcerned that I was following him. As I closed the gap between us, a man in his pajamas stepped outside his front door to get the newspaper.

He looked squarely at me, behind me, ahead of me, and then shouted, "Is that your deer?"

Before I could respond, he slammed the door with great deliberation, taking cover indoors. The buck didn't break stride as I closed the distance between us. He dropped a little bundle of scat, the sole indication of his feelings. Down the block, a toddler glimpsed us through his screen door, swung the pacifier hanging by a ribbon from his neck in a little circle, smacked his hands on the glass of his front door, and shrieked.

His mother came up behind him, snatched him back by the elbows, opened her door and shouted the same question, "Is that your deer?"

I didn't reply. Did she want me to leash and drag him back to my fenced yard?

Has she seen the large herd of deer that uses our elaborately marked trail system to travel from one foraging ground to another? They don't vote or pay taxes. Yet they snack on newly planted shrubs, ambitious vegetable gardens, and succulent saplings. They yard up and bed down undisturbed. Their prints appear in sand and snow all over town.

Deer in the city is a controversial subject. Recently, in a residential park, a deer was shot with a rifle at 7 am and hauled away by the DNR. How this happened is debatable, but many residents find deer to be a nuisance.

Elizabeth Marshall Thomas' *The Hidden Life of Deer* describes deer's wild ways. Thomas tracked, fed, and studied deer for years. I learned a lot about their habits, but nothing about how to control them. Curiosity piqued, I sought further instruction by reading her other work. In The *Hidden Life of Dogs*, Thomas described a pack of dingo-husky dogs, their trails, and urination habits. She never confined her "pack" at home, and sometimes shacked up with them both indoors and outdoors. When Thomas detailed how she allowed mice and rats into her home, all in the interest of science, I decided she was two tacos short of a combination plate even though she might be an interesting guest at a dinner party. That ended my brief research and I was still stuck with the question.

Deer in the city are increasingly common, as are turkeys, rabbits, and coyotes. They're hungry, unruly, and messy. They drop their perfect little pellets everywhere. Until we find a peaceful, compassionate alternative to our cohabitation, the accurate answer to "Is that your deer?" is "Yes."

Katy's Farm

Katy's husband Jim was seated comfortably on his rotary tractor (he called it a "bush hog"), cap over his eyes, moving steadily along, calm and quiet except for the whir of the blades. He could have been any farmer out minding his field, the hum of blades mowing and churning, scattering hay back and forth on the five hundred plus acre farm. He mowed the hay in even, parallel rows, bent on the task before him, without hesitation. The field sloped down to the Shenandoah River, and behind that stretched the gentle curves of the Blue Ridge Mountains.

Jim was dependable and regular as the beating hearts of the women who sat in a circle at poolside, waiting to be lulled into the belief that God's in his heaven, all's right with the world. Glasses of chablis in hand, they forgot for a while their lives as teachers in a disordered environment. It was tempered now by the joy of being together, away from town, away from conflict, away from responsibility. The country's blissful ambiance melted away their shared agitation.

Katy invited them to wind down on Friday afternoon after a long week filled with children who suffer from too much violence and technology and too little parenting. Peg and Lucy and Carol and Katy all worked together in an

elementary school in Virginia. Carol and Lucy and Peg had never really been in the country like this and they were thrilled to be invited to Katy and Jim's farm, far away from whiteboards and conferences, calming the frenzy in their spirits.

Soothed and warmed by the setting sun, dipping their bodies from time to time in her swimming pool, sipping their wine, admiring the wheat-colored grasses falling softly, randomly, from the blades of the tractor, vulnerable, needy children were the farthest things from their minds. They relaxed wordlessly, squinting at the yellow orb lowering in the sky. They listened to the springy whistling of orioles, peepers in the marshes, the rush of water from the Shenandoah River, and the regular rhythm of the tractor moving back and forth across the field. Rain had washed away winter's afterbirth to make room for fresh green.

Katy and her husband knew the ways of the country. They offered their understanding of the beauty of the world to friends in the way they knew how, by simply sharing its gifts.

As the women settled into late-day conversation, sliding easily from one subject to another, sinking into the comforting hum of their own voices, inhaling the verdant freshly-cut grass; suddenly, there was a loud thud, a whirring of blades, and then a slight pause, while the collective hearts of the women skipped a beat. As teachers, they were accustomed to interruptions, aware that any shift in sound could indicate a situation they may have to control. Katy held her breath, familiar with the sound they all heard, knowing what it meant. The women, unaware of her subtle change, resumed their conversations, lying back on the chaises lounges, pulling their chairs into a tighter circle to hear one another. Jim pressed the gearshift forward and continued his work, braiding his way across the pasture, in long, even patterns, down and back across the acreage.

Katy sat up, her eyes growing wide as she studied a particular spot her husband left in the field, a small crater, barely discernible except to the trained eye. The other women, sensing trouble, sat up too and watched her for clues since they didn't know where else to look.

A doe raced to the field, her nose smelling the spot Katy had her eye on. As soon as Jim turned the tractor back toward the spot, the doe ran away to the edge of the field. Jim mowed next to the spot, his lines straight and careful. He continued on, down the line, and then turned the blades back again to make a new line. The doe returned. This time, other females joined her and formed a radial spoke around the spot where the crack sounded. Their noses were down, sniffing. Some were alert to Jim, watching him until he turned back again toward the spot. As soon as he did, they fled into the trees. When he turned his back to them again, they returned, reforming the circle.

The women gripped their wine glasses. Carol swallowed hard, Lucy whimpered quietly. Peg asked questions: "Katy, what happened? What was the terrible noise? Why were the deer there? Did one of them get run over?"

"A fawn," Katy said. "It must have been a fawn. Sometimes mother deer hide them deep in the grass, especially after giving birth. Their hooves are barely hardened, so they can't run yet."

There was no other way to tell them. Their eyes and ears were virgin to the ways of a farm. It was hard for them to accept, but it was also hard for Katy.

Carol brought her hand to her mouth and with her lips drawn down, sobbed softly into her cocktail napkin. Peg and Lucy looked at each other, dismayed. "Is there something we can do?"

Katy's face was sad, but clear. "No," she said, standing up to observe the small crowd of turkey vultures rising up on air currents to circle the spot. "Look…see that? That means the fawn is already gone."

All three women stood up too, scraping back their lounge chairs, joining Katy at the fence facing the spot. "Gone?"

"I mean dead."

"Did your husband know what he did?"

"Yes, I think so."

"And he just -?"

"Yes," said Katy.

"Ohmigod, how awful."

"The vultures are so ugly."

The women studied the curved shoulders and red heads of the vultures. They looked like skulking caricatures of birds of prey, like Snoopy on the roof of his doghouse pretending to be Red Baron. "Yes, but it's part of the cycle…" Katy's voice was reassuring and folksy, rhythmic as a well-worn rocking chair, dependable as a wedding ring quilt, familiar as the music of Aaron Copland.

The does returned to the scene, taking their places again, as if preordained. Their radial pattern dissected the long straight rows of the tilled field. They were forming a kind of Nazca line—a mysterious bond—around the fawn and its mother.

"What are the deer doing?" Peg asked Katy.

"I don't know. Let's watch and see if we can figure it out," said Katy. Teachers are highly suggestible. This was their country lesson, a real one, one they didn't plan, one they'd never forget. They wanted to go home, but they wanted to stay to witness the events unfolding. Pouring themselves more wine, they felt colder now. They were restless as the does, searching for a way to restore the scene to its former calm. But they lacked the does' communal intuition. They were unable to console each other. Sunset bled into the sky, leaking into lavender-blue.

The vultures spread their wings, rocking from side to side, barely flapping, in a circular pattern.

"I wish I had binoculars," Carol said.

Without warning, out from behind the mountains, like a bolt of lightning, a bald eagle pierced the sky. It swooped down, fastened its talons to the body of the fawn and lifted the entire animal into the air. The women gasped. The eagle carried the heavy package with its four drooping hooves, out through a hole in the distant heaven, deserting the vultures, the crowd of keening does, the mother deer, the assemblage of female teachers, Katy, her husband Jim, and the farm.

Carol and Lucy and Peg turned to face each other, shaking their heads.

"I'm sorry," said Katy.

Leaving their wine glasses by the pool, gathering their scattered clothes and belongings, one by one, they muttered a hasty goodbye to Katy for an afternoon it didn't feel right to thank her for, but knew they must escape immediately. Weaving toward their cars, they contemplated how today's events would fit into their nature lesson on life cycles, but for now, it seemed urgent to get home. Home through traffic, home to the six o'clock news, home where they could control the spectacle of life and death with the slight finger pressure of a remote control. On. Off.

Cow and Bull Stories

I. A GOOD MAN

It was late November, cold and rainy enough to make the Shenandoah River high and the current fast. The Blue Ridge Mountains ran like an endless melody up the valley, and from time to time, when no one seemed to be paying any attention, threw down heavy boulders that settled in the river bottom as if they'd been there all along.

Jim fed the cows from the back of his pickup, but couldn't see his favorite, Beatrice. She had a way of hanging around the margins of the herd, so when she plodded away, he didn't see her.

A black Angus like the rest, she had a strong head and girth, but it was her temperament that had Jim's heart. She never balked or shied away. When he threw out feed, she'd stroll up to him, shove her huge head right under his elbow and nod, asking for a scratch behind the ears. She looked up at him in a way that was smarter than any yard dog he'd ever known. She calmed him. In turn, he spoiled her, called her Bea, and gave her more attention than he gave anybody, including family. They had a mutual trust. She was sweet, gentle and productive, a big ol' gal who'd borne him ten prize calves.

When Jim realized Bea was missing, he hurried down to the river because he'd seen her amble off in that direction the night before. The medicine he gave Bea for the skin infection made her thirsty and uncomfortable, and it was likely she wanted to cool down. He thought he'd heard her bellowing.

Sure enough, there she was, up past her shoulders in the Shenandoah. With her dark head among the shadows of overhanging trees, it was hard to tell her from a giant boulder that had tumbled down the mountains. He didn't see as well as he did in his twenties. He yelled at her, "Bea! Beatrice! Now you come out from there. Don't make me go in and get you. It's damned cold and I haven't got my waders on."

Jim could see she wasn't moving much and guessed she'd gotten stuck in the mud, paralyzed from cold. She was snorting and gasping for air, the whites of her eyes large, trying to keep her head out of water. Like Ophelia, she was "incapable of her own distress." Even if he could toss a rope round her neck, he'd throw out his back trying to pull her from the muck.

He was studying the situation when he heard voices upstream. He jogged alongshore until he spied two people paddling a canoe around the bend, heading right toward Bea. Close up, he recognized his father, J.C., and his brother Charlie's girl, Ruth.

"Hello!" he shouted. "Careful now, Dad. Just ahead, Beatrice is stuck in the mud in the middle of the river. You'll have to go around her or stop right where you are."

"You say Bea's stuck? Hell, boy, I can get her out. We

just put in a few hundred yards away. I've got steam left in me yet."

"She's too big. Looks like she's in the mud pretty good. I don't think either one of us can get her out," Jim said.

"Don't worry, Jim. We'll get 'er out."

"No, Gramps, please!" cried the girl, shrilly.

Jim watched helplessly as his father paddled hard and swung the canoe straight toward Beatrice. Then, with the flat of his paddle, he splashed water on her face, right between her eyes.

Lord God! What the hell is he doing? Jim thought. Beatrice startled, struggled to turn away. Her eyes were rolling and she let out a big bellow. Next came the moment Jim, to this day, can't believe. Beatrice, all 1735 pounds of her, lifted her front hooves up out of the river muck and clambered to get into the canoe. Hoof after hoof.

Poor ole Bea. Poor gal. She's all confused. I let her think she could count on me. I let her down.

Jim couldn't get into the river in time. Bea was going to kill them all.

Jim shouted, "Let it go! Steer your canoe away! Fast!" He waded into the river, taking big steps.

"I'll handle it! I'll handle it!" said the old man.

Bea set her ears back, flared her nostrils, and with all her remaining strength, raised her hooves up, punching a hole right through the canoe.

The river, churned with hooves, arms, legs and splintered pieces of wood. The old man's visor cap floated away; the girl's long red hair came loose from its elastic band and streamed around her like algae. Bea was bawling. Only her huge head was above water now—eyes bulging.

The old man extended his paddle out to the cow, helplessly. In a matter of seconds, it was only Bea's black ears, a huge black hulk sinking, and then nothing.

"She's underwater!" Jim's voice caught. "Dad! Hang on to that big chunk of canoe next to you!" Jim stripped off his jacket, and yanked off his shoes and socks. He threw them on shore and dived into the icy water, paddling against the swirling current. He reached for his father, threw his arm around his chest and dragged his frail body to shore. Chloe had already swum to shore. She covered her mouth with her hands and watched, shivering and crying. Jim dragged J.C. out of the river and dropped him on the bank, pulling his arms out of the sleeves of his sodden green parka.

J.C.'s face was weathered with deep ruts, like a dried-up riverbed, and tough as hide. His jaw was locked with determined ferocity, its intensity matched only by Chloe's. Her face was sprinkled with freckles, a bright galaxy strewn with stars.

He threw the girl the keys to his truck. "Start it up and turn on the heat all the way to high!"

"What about Beatrice?"

"I'm sure Dad meant well, but it looks like Bea's gone. This time for good. Whatever strength she had left, she used up. It's best not to interfere with some things." *There's never a right time with the ones you love.*

The broken-off bow of the canoe was caught on a fallen tree, looking like it might break free with the next current, shard of a misguided mission.

"I'm going in for the rest of the canoe. Gramps got that canoe so we could go on trips." Before Jim could stop her, the girl was in the water again, khaki pants and light jacket clinging to her skin. She could barely lift her legs but as soon as she was over her head, she swam right to the canoe and grabbed a broken-off fragment, nearly three-quarters of the canoe. Its gunwales intact, she maneuvered it in front of her ashore, while Jim brought the old man to his truck and lifted him into the front of the cab. Jim buried him under woolen blankets, crusty with clods of earth and prickly hay, the ones he used to warm up sick and new born calves. He remembered wrapping Bea in it as a newborn calf. The old man nodded off. Jim reached under the front seat, pulled out a small flask of whiskey, took a swig, and coaxed J.C.'s lips open, tipping his face up to make him drink. The old man sputtered and coughed. Jim got out of the truck one last time to see if he could find Bea. He squatted and peered down into the rough, striped current, hoping, still hoping. He found his jacket and shoes, turned to smile weakly at Chloe, steeling himself. The two of them lifted the broken canoe up to the top of his truck where he tied down the awkward, useless shape with twine. They trembled in the chilly air, finding it hard to feel their fingers and toes. It began to sleet.

"Get in front," he said to the girl, "on the other side of your grandfather, and I'll take you home."

She put one arm around her grandfather. The other hand she placed on her belly.

The old man's mouth was agape, in a zone between sleep and wakefulness, the one where life clings to itself, where words are a faint buzz.

"Grandma's picking us up at the boat access. Gramps makes me really mad sometimes. Once he gets his mind fixed on something, you just can't change it. I tried to get him to stop."

"It's not your fault, Chloe."

"Gramps'll be sad she didn't make it. I'm home for Thanksgiving. They shut down the dorms and Dad didn't want me home."

"Why not?" Jim said, blasting the heat.

"I thought if I got back into the cold water, maybe... Uncle Jim? I'm going to name my daughter after Bea, if that's okay with you."

Jim looked over and frowned at the girl. Her face was ruddy from the exertion of swimming in the cold. It was then, with her clothing heavy and wet around her body, that he noticed the small swelling in her belly. "Gramps is the only one speaking to me. Grandma's mad and Dad says, 'You have your whole life in front of you. Get rid of it. Close the chapter.' Like my life is a book. Easy for him to say. I'm going to bring her up better than I was brought up." A kind of throaty sob came from somewhere deep inside her. He was afraid to look at her.

"Your dad's a good man. So's your grandfather," Jim said. "They do their best. That's all any of us can do. Can't think of too many who'd risk their lives for a head of livestock. Beatrice had no business wading into the river. She got in over her head. Sorry to lose her. Sick and sorry."

The girl was gasping for breath now, her body rocking back and forth. Soon, she gave in to loud sobs.

Jim was remembering Beatrice's birth. He'd had to use a chain to pull her out. Her head was so big, it got stuck in the birth canal. She was glossy and wet, but full of herself.

She wobbled to her feet and suckled immediately. He'd felt a surge of feeling, he guessed he could call it love. He named her after his favorite aunt, whose independent spirit impressed him.

"Is Gramps gonna make it?" the girl said between sobs. "What if he gets pneumonia?"

Jim looked at J.C.'s faded face. He started the ignition, wiping off steam inside the windshield, turning on the wipers, and glancing one last time at the Shenandoah. He backed up slowly, reluctantly, and turned away from the river where he'd last seen Bea. She was black and shiny as wet mud and the river was dark. He'd never spot her now.

"Is he gonna die?" Her voice changed to a wail.

"There are no guarantees. Didn't anyone ever tell you that? Why, Beatrice might've had years left. Or she could have died tomorrow. No one knows." He could feel his temper rising. Then, softening, Jim said, "Anyway, Beatrice is a good name." He tucked Chloe under the chin. "Just about as fine a name as she could have." Jim was grateful his own kids were grown and settled. He pulled into the access parking lot. Barely visible above the steering wheel of the old, red, Chevy pickup, was Ruth, his mother, who clambered down to the running board. Without climbing down to the puddled ground, she peered at them through fogged glasses, puzzled.

Chloe turned to Jim and kissed him on the cheek. "Thanks, Uncle Jim."

"It's your choice, Chloe. Your daughter will grow up strong as you," Jim said. "Teach her from the beginning. Teach her everything." Then he added, "Teach her to swim."

II. TAKING THE BULL BY THE HORNS

Charlie talked low and easy to him, "Settle down, now, Pluto, just take it easy. We'll be done with this whole business before you know it."

"Toss him a bale of hay," his father, J.C., said, observing the proceedings from the cab of Charlie's truck. "He's too much, that one. A bull shouldn't have a personality. I didn't build up this cattle ranch just for fun, boy. I had you two in mind. Just fatten 'em up and sell 'em off. Surest formula," J.C. stood for James Charles and clarified who was who. Charlie's older brother Jim got the other half of J. C's name and raised cows on the nearby acreage.

"Okay, Dad," Charlie said. Charlie brought J.C. along to break up his routine of oatmeal and meds that the average morning brought. J.C. liked to remind Charlie that he was the one who started the ranching outfit fifty years ago. Eighty years old and proud.

Through pasture gates, the lowering sun striped the grasses, turned aspen leaves lemon, and sugar maples tangerine. Charlie was readying to haul nine thousand pounds of bovine flesh to Fairfax Community Agricultural College. His experience, skill and life story made him the best man around to teach about marketing bulls.

He was sure he'd eliminated previous years' mistakes by picking bulls with enough contrast to clearly define Dollar Value Indices, or DVI. Many of the graduate students were adults with some ranching experience behind them, but some were townies with big ideas and little judgment.

Charlie led his six choice bulls up the trailer ramp when Pluto, the last, wagged his head and rolled his eyes. Pluto was too smart is all, and sensed it was no ordinary day. Intelligence is not an asset to breeding stock. Charlie's attempts to breed brains out of the herd failed when it came to Pluto.

"Son, why in hell is it necessary to bring six bulls? Two's plenty. Three's two hands full. Four's a belly full and five is more than one man should handle in public. But six is plain asking for trouble."

"Dad, I explained before. These kids, well, some are way older than kids, these students need to see contrast to measure DVI. Otherwise, all bulls look the same to them. I need Riga who's sired some beautiful beef. Silas and Jupiter, well, they're just good lookin' animal flesh. Shogun's hefty as hell, and Biggun has the most impressive scrotum in the county. Downright magnificent. Pluto. My big boy. The best bull a market could afford."

"I see, son. Well, sure glad I asked. I guess I got my answer then."

Ruth, his mother, liked J.C. to have a good airing once a week, like the sheets. J.C. was amiable, unless Charlie took into account his unsolicited advice.

Charlie pulled out of the long driveway and began the drive to the campus mall. J.C. sat in the passenger seat, refusing to fasten his seat belt. "Hell, I've lived this long, flapping around loose, I won't strangle to death now!" J.C. alternately hummed and dozed off until they reached Fairfax.

A group of students were milling about, watching, as Charlie pulled his trailer up to the curb. He cut a good figure—tall, lean, and a little bit shy. Feathers of gray at his temples made them feel mature as they pictured themselves seated across from him at the worn oak kitchen table, sipping black coffee, morning sun rosying their cheeks. Rumor had it Charlie Dodge had a daughter almost their age, off to college somewhere in the Midwest. They also knew he was eligible, successful, and handsome as hell. More than one coed secretly imagined herself lassoed and ravished.

He stepped out to shake the hand of Lance Nelson, F.C.C.'s Agricultural marketing instructor. After hastily setting up a makeshift fence, Charlie led each bull out, one by one, down the ramp. He brought Riga out first, tied him up, and then brought out Pluto, nodding and yanking at the rope. Charlie kept up a patter of introductory information for the students, hoping Pluto would settle down. "These are all Angus bulls. Brought over here from Scotland in 1883 and represent the largest beef breed registry association in the world. These boys are fine specimens of the breed. Riga, for starters, born in 1981, has a great EPD. Y'all know what an EPD is, right? It stands for Expected Progeny Differences. A lot of monograms in this business. I'll throw 'em out and explain 'em once."

Charlie tossed hay under Pluto's nose. "Here now, boy, settle down." Charlie chuckled. "Wanted to save him to last, but he can be a little cantankerous if I don't pay him enough attention. Too smart for his own good." Charlie went back to Riga, trying to distract them from Pluto's restlessness.

Some students clustered around, making notes. They'd been raised around animals and liked the smell of cowhide. Others, eyes round, backed up slightly from the fence, fidgeting with their clipboards.

Charlie went on. "As I was saying EPD is Expected Progeny Difference or prediction of its calves relative to other Angus, see? We can expect Riga will sire some strong calves. You might want to take notes. Pay attention to Riga's conformation. Top Angus should be well-muscled all over."

He brought out another bull and tied him up. "Shogun here, now he rates top CW or carcass weight. Pound for pound he's like gold ingot." He led out three more bulls. "Now, Biggun's got a good package. Notice his height and SC compared to the other animals you see here." Charlie scanned the crowd. He went ahead anyway. "SC stands for scrotal circumference. It means a lot to folks in this business. You gals better get used to it. Compare him to Pluto." Pluto raised his head on cue, responding to his name.

"Calm down now, Pluto. He gets excited in unfamiliar situations. Bulls can be touchy. You don't want to get 'em riled." Charlie threw out more hay to keep all six of them busy.

"So, you got Pluto, Riga, Shogun, Biggun, Jupiter, and Silas. Each eartag documents the bull's registration number, whose bull he is, when he was born and who sired him. Jupiter and Silas have excellent overall DVI's. Can anyone tell me what that means?" He kept a close eye as they flicked tails and stomped hooves.

One gal raised her hand straight up. No hesitancy. When Charlie didn't notice, she blurted out, "Sir...?"

"Call me Charlie," said Charlie, watching Pluto out of the corner of one eye.

"Charlie, sir, DVI is Dollar Value Index. But what I think we need, that is, what I'd like to know is about current market prices. What are they like right now? Are they down or up?"

"Actually, Miss..."

"My name's Joann."

"What's that? You'll have to excuse me. Got kicked in the head once or twice and lost a bit of hearing," Charlie said.

"Joann? My name's Joann." The girl broke through the small crowd and crooked her arms over the fence, looking right at Charlie, so close he could smell the peppermint lifesaver she was sucking. Her rosebud lips puckered as she watched him intently. J.C. watched the proceedings from the side view mirror, still hoping Charlie would find a match. His divorce from Denise made him edgy. She'd been nothing but trailer trash who wrangled him into marriage by getting herself knocked up. When she ran off with that s.o.b. from godknowswhere, she got what she deserved. He and Ruth did what they could to bring up the girl, but she was lost. What Jim needed was a good woman's soothing touch and some help around the ranch. A woman with sense.

"Well, Joann, there are some things I can't answer. Each bull has an ACC or accuracy index. Another one of them monograms."

"Acronyms," said Joann, smiling at him, confidence growing.

"Monograms, anagrams, whatever you call it, I can't predict their worth off the top of my head. Market place is fickle as a woman." A few titters bubbled up.

"As I understand it, part of your training is to calculate answers yourselves."

"I'd rather hear it from you, Charlie," Joann said, looking directly into his eyes.

Charlie felt an old, but familiar longing. "All right, Joann." He cleared his throat and went on. "Make a habit of listening to the livestock reports every morning. That way it'll come more naturally to you. Just think of me as a rancher who was lucky enough to grow up in the cattle business. Mind your books and you'll do better than I when it's your turn." Laughter erupted now and spread through the small crowd of students.

"No sense being modest, Charlie," said Lance. "Give them a forecast…"

"Nyah. You know me better'n that. I like to be right."

One of the townies in the audience, Tom, had heard cattle ranching would pay more than trucking, and thought if he looked the part of a cowboy, he'd become one. His pants were so tight, you could see which side of the zipper his member chose to rest behind. Curious, Tom leaned over and stroked the big bull's sweaty black hide. Silas jerked his big head around and left a trail of snot that snaked down the front of Tom's new, stone-washed Levi jacket, Tom recoiled, laughed a little too loud, and reached into his back pocket. Shaking out a crisp yellow bandanna, he made a show of wiping his jacket.

"What an idiot!" said Joann, in a loud voice.

Maybe it was the bandanna. Maybe it was the laughter that caught on like brush fire when Tom screwed up his face. Witnesses saw it as if it were in slow motion.

First, the fence started to chatter. Charlie's expression shifted to a frown. J.C. sat up in the truck. Pluto placed one hoof onto the flimsy fence and pushed it over, snapping a couple of the slatted boards like toothpicks. He stepped over the now-splintered enclosure, strutting with a steady bouncing gait, until he understood there was nothing keeping him in. When he realized he had absolute and complete release for the first time in his life, he bolted, pell-mell, up the campus mall.

Tom, intent on regaining his image, gathered his awkward limbs under him and took off after him. Rick and Dwight and several of the other young men followed. A herd of college students, joined the crowd, chasing Pluto, fancying themselves in Pamplona.

Pluto's tail and head were up, as he ran, stiff-legged, down the tree-lined quadrangle of stately buildings. Excited and afraid, Pluto shat out all the hay Charlie had fed him behind the fence, in the trailer and in pasture the day before, shat it out in a series of steaming piles down the mall.

Past the Physics building, past Chemistry, Journalism, English, Languages, the library, the Student Union, past clumps of students who were seated on the grass, who locked their eyes on the four-legged bull, clattering down the pavement. It didn't take him long to clear the entire campus grounds. Pluto was bent on freedom and headed for parts unknown.

Soon he reached the outskirts of campus at County Road H. By then, the college men had quit the chase, leaning over their bent knees, gasping for air, over the trail of excreta. Tom and Dwight gazed into the distance, squinting to see if Pluto was still in sight.

"Damned near caught him," Tom said.

"You weren't even close, dude," Dwight said.

"If you hadn't gotten in my way, I woulda had him for sure," Tom said, smiling.

Dwight took a pretend swing at Tom and Tom put up an arm in defense.

A farmer on his tractor was chugging along the road when Pluto skidded around him, avoiding the slough below. The farmer looked none too happy. Pluto, with cows on his mind, took a sharp right, into the nearest yard, where Judy McCallum was hanging out wash on the line. Pluto trotted right between the legs of Mert's overalls, still wet enough to slap the bull in the face and leave him glistening. Pluto continued on, pulling the clothesline with him around his chest. Right through her garden, with no regard for the delicate leaves of Bibb lettuce that peeped up limey through brown earth, smashing them flat, or her prize dahlias, whose yellow blooms had reached the size of plates. All was crushed beneath the heat of Pluto's hooves. One end of the clothesline slipped to the ground between Pluto's left leg, and the other glued to his right front hoof, with wet soil from Judy McCallum's recently watered garden. The line snapped free, but a hint of pink lace remained wrapped around Pluto's leg, annoying him. He paused long enough to remove it with his horn, where it draped itself and hung down like a flag.

Back at the college, Charlie, muttering an apology, hastily packed up Shogun, Silas, Biggun, Riga and Jupiter in the trailer. J.C, puzzled and disappointed, dozed off again. When Charlie lurched the truck into drive and gave chase, J.C.'s forehead slammed back and then forward right into the front windshield.

"Dad, you gotta strap up now. Pluto's broken loose!"

"Well, let's go then! I ain't hurt, son. Just get a move on after him before he gets hit by a semi heading for Indiana," Charlie rubbed his forehead.

Joann stood to one side, waving shyly, as Charlie pulled away. He touched the brim of his hat and nodded, truck tires kicking up dust and spitting small stones.

"Well, looks like you got more than you bargained for, son. You got a little gal all excited, thinking you were what she'd been waiting for all of her young life, and then you left her in the dust. Top of that, your prize bull, who was going to help you demonstrate your true skill as a cattle man, shot off down the road and may get himself into a hell of a jam before you're likely to catch him."

Charlie regretted taking his father. "I know what you're thinking, Dad. Pluto's no prize. He gets himself into predicaments 'cause he doesn't mind his own business. But, a bull has to learn his place, like the rest of us."

"Who taught you to think like that? You can't teach a bull anything. They're nothing but big, stubborn, horny animals. That's where the expression "bull-headed" came from, son." J. C. paused and cleared his throat. "I spent my life trying to outwit them and came to find out that all that time they had no wits. Well, for Lord's sake, give chase, boy," J.C. said, chuckling.

"If we're lucky, Pluto will use his GPS system," Charlie said.

"I'm not certain what you mean by that, but hell, a good dog'll find his way home," J.C. said. "Let's hope he's that smart. It's getting close to suppertime."

Trucks zoomed past them both ways as they pulled out onto the shoulder. It was Friday when truckers hurry to get their shipments delivered before the weekend.

Scanning the road for signs of Pluto, Charlie tried to determine how far a bull could walk or run by the time Charlie and J.C. drove down the highway. On a hunch, Charlie pulled into the driveway of a little rambler. A pickup was parked by the front door, so Charlie threw his truck into park and hopped out. J.C.'s forehead bounced forward again. From around the side of the house, a man in his late fifties limped heavily toward him, head down. He held a pitchfork in one hand and a rake in the other.

"What can I do for you?" said the man.

Charlie kept it brief. "This is a strange question, but have you seen a bull down the road?"

"No, sir, can't say as I have."

"All right, then, thanks anyway."

"What should I do if I see him?" the man said.

"Chase him home!" Charlie said, already back in the truck, yelling out of his window.

"Where's home?"

"Just chase him. He knows where to go!"

"Is he running away?" the man said.

Charlie jerked the truck into gear. "You might say that. Running from too many questions."

The man took off his cap, scratched his head and squinted up at Charlie. Charlie noticed a long deep scar, high up below his hairline, running clear across, as if his scalp had torn away. "I could throw a rope around his neck. I've had a little experience in my day. Used to ride bulls."

"I wouldn't be averse to your trying, if you think you could do it." Charlie said, looking the man up and down, from unlaced steel-toed boots to faded red plaid shirt hanging out of threadbare jeans, "but I wouldn't try hopping on his back."

"I'll watch out for him. Angus, right?"

"Yup. Big one. Too smart for his own good."

J.C. let out a guffaw. He was having more fun than he bargained for on this trip. That bull was giving his boy a run for his money. Charlie'd found a woman. Hell, it took him 'til he was forty to meet Ruth. Jim married at twenty-two, and stayed married, but Charlie married Denise still wet behind the ears.

"Thanks a lot, Mister...?" Charlie said.

"Ty, Ty Torrance."

"I'm Charlie. This is my father, James Charles Dodge. Think we'll chase around after him until the other bulls in the back start to object, or until I can find some trace of him, whichever comes first."

"Aw, maybe he's in a corn field somewhere, having himself a feast," Ty said.

"Far as I'm concerned that darned bull is ready for market. Charlie here spends too much time chasing the bulls around. Should be chasing skirt," J.C. said. "Say, seen any good-lookin' women around?"

Ty scratched his head. "Not really, unless you mean my late wife, but I guess you can't see her now, can ya?" Ty let out a whoop and slapped his thigh. "I'll keep a lookout, just in case."

Charlie cranked the steering wheel around and drove back down the highway and raised his index finger to touch his hat, indicating thanks to Ty. In the back of the truck, five bulls were banging around. Charlie's sudden starts and stops were throwing them off balance.

J.C. rubbed his head, where a small knot was growing. "Say, boy, you better slow your pace a little. Those prized bulls of yours will be hard to coax up the ramp on the next go around. And you don't want to run him down before you get a chance to give him a piece of your mind."

Charlie turned in on County Road I, about ten miles from home. Had he been in less of a hurry, he would've seen Pluto a little earlier, shuffling along down County Road H, toward Ty's place, one hoof wrapped in clothesline, one horn adorned with a strip of pink panties.

Ty anticipated Pluto's path, and stood in the road holding the heaviest rope he could find, tied into a lasso. He faced the setting sun, breathing in the rusty-rich smell of late corn, feeling strength in the palms of his weathered hands coming back to life. He gripped the coarse fibers, feeling the pull. As he tied the rope around his gut, his scrotum recalled the rockhard rhythm of the bull. His shoulders remembered the brickblunt press of the earth. His ribs remembered the cracks, ripping around his chest.

When he spotted Pluto, lumbering down the road, Ty stepped into the shadows, watched, and waited.

Pluto snorted and stopped in his tracks. Around the bend, a milk truck sped along, its long silver cylinders glinting in the sun. Seeing the bull, the driver honked his horn, pulled out into the wrong lane, laying rubber, and almost tipped trying to avoid Pluto, who took off in a run.

Ty's blood coursed through his veins with fresh speed as he took off in pursuit. A few circular tosses over his head and he'd have him. The truck spit sand in his eyes, making him miss the first toss. One more loop and he had the bull by the horns. He'd forgotten how strong an Angus could be. Pluto dragged him down the road. Ty felt every day of his fifty-three years in his joints as he sprang into action.

Loosening up the rope, he circled around a big oak tree until Pluto came to the end of his rope, about ten yards. Ty waited for the right moment to start pulling and tightening the rope to haul the bull in. Pluto strained at the end of the rope for a long time before changing his mind and twisting around in the other direction to come after Ty.

Ty was ready. He stood close enough to the oak tree to lure the bull toward him. Pluto and Ty chased each other around the tree a few times until the rope tightened around Pluto's neck. Ty had him. He tied a good knot with the ends of the rope and ran for cover. Ty had outsmarted Pluto, but he also knew his bulls. Pluto wasn't near tired enough to call it quits. Panting hard and fast, straining against the rope, the bull charged. Ty would have to call a vet to shoot a few tranquilizing darts at him so he could loosen the rope around his head, and lead him back into the truck.

As the seven o'clock sun lowered, Pluto stood his ground, losing air, eyes bulging, pink panties around his horns, bits of clothesline clinging to his tail, and a lasso around his neck.

Ty studied his quarry. The bull was licked. Ty rubbed his palms together until blood rushed back into his hands. Limb by limb, he coaxed and rubbed his body back to life. He stomped his feet until his knees stopped shivering. Soon he felt the full length of his legs.

Ty heard the rumble of a truck that sounded like the one Charlie was driving. He swallowed the lump in the back of his throat, stood up straight, chest puffed out a little, the way he used to strut in the rodeo ring. He squinted down the road, spotting the two men in the cab of the truck, grateful he could still toss a pretty good rope.

Out of the corner of his eye, Charlie saw a slash of pink, reminding him of the last time he bedded down with a woman. That young gal Joann had brains, guts and conformation. Fact was her overall DVI was solid. She might even be a help to Chloe. What started out as an embarrassment was turning into a fine day. In fact, it was downright promising. Might even make J.C. proud.

Forced Entry

I

When he got out of the pen, it was the only job at the mall where they didn't ask questions. It wasn't his type of work, but he stayed because of her, because of the one who would solve his problems, teach him how to make it in the world, the world outside this cage.

He couldn't get any of it right—even the damned tie. Either the skinny end or the fat end hung down below his belt. It was embarrassing when no one else seemed to have any trouble getting both ends to match up. He tucked the long end of his tie into his pants so it didn't flip out over the counter when he waited on a customer. He hoped no one would notice.

He agreed to tie his long hair into a rubber band so it didn't fall into the developing fluids. But he flaunted his hoop earring and saved the dangling one for Mondays when his manager was there. He figured if the Man made a fuss, he could fuckin' file for discrimination.

The button-down shirt was no problem but the tight khakis got stuck up his ass and made him look like a geek. Why did they make him wear this freak outfit? No one wore a navy-blue tie with red polka dots anymore. Not even corporates. He felt bound up and gagged.

II

She hated it when there was a line, especially if the other customers were ordering reprints. They'd hem and haw and not quite be able to decide which print it was they wanted to duplicate. She was feeling tired and wanted to get out and run. She'd been hurrying from the time she got up until she got home, when she stripped off her work clothes, threw on her running gear, grabbed the dogs and ran out the door without taking time to tie her shoes. She was excited to see how the shots from her last trip to Canada turned out. It had been incredibly beautiful to swim in glacial waters. Every pore opened, swelled and froze in place, shocking her. She stretched her arms and legs into the icy black until she no longer felt her body. Her arms became scoops, churning and splashing faster and faster until she thought her heart would puncture her chest. When she could no longer stand the piercing pleasure, she broke from the water for her clothes, her nipples hard as bullets, her whole body alive in exquisite pain. Suddenly, she remembered there was a shot of her in the nude and felt weird to think one of the photo guys developing it, able to handle her soul in a 4x6, touch its edges.

III

There she was, just behind the woman at the counter. He was blinded by her shining blonde hair, flyaway, partly tucked into the collar of her royal blue jacket. Her face was flushed, like she'd been running. A tee-shirt hung out over her shorts. Her running shoes were untied. He smelled her perfume, dampened by sweat. Like roses. Like fuckin' roses.

The woman ahead of her set her baby on the high counter and let go of him completely while she wrote out a check. If that baby had turned around or wiggled at all, it could have broken its arms, legs and its little baby skull. He couldn't decide if the mother had some great knowledge about babies or was just stupid. He decided she was stupid and watched, holding his breath, as she signed her name. The baby turned slightly to watch the pen move across the check. He watched the baby's chubby feet dangle helplessly out over the four-foot counter. He wanted to rush out from behind the counter and rescue him from his mother.

But, that wasn't the thing to do. He knew that. The woman he had waited for was right behind her. He couldn't risk moving away from the counter for a moment. The stupid mother finally paid, hooked her baby onto her hip, shoved her photos into her purse and left.

And then she was up, the one who stirred his pulse to a rhythm so rapid he thought his wrists would burst. He looked at her, hoping she would show some sign of recognition, but she threw the roll on the counter and greeted the customer next to her. The man started yammering about his mother's bypass, his wife and kids. She acted like she couldn't wait to leave.

IV

Saved by the guy in the uniform. She hated running into her neighbor. He represented everything she despised. She tried to sound sincere when she asked about his family, but she hadn't learned her lesson yet, the one about holding your own force intact and private, about being quiet. As usual, he told her way more detail than she cared to know, about his mother's bypass, his children's soccer awards. She nodded, not listening, and put in her order with the guy at the counter.

V

His voice trembled as he asked for her phone number, whether she wanted 4 by 6 or 3 by 5, matte or glossy, and an extra set, even though he knew her answers by heart. 4 by 6 glossy, extra set, was her usual order, except when she brought in the ones she liked. She took the negatives out of a white envelope, held them up to the light instead of using the light table on the counter. His eyes followed one drop of sweat crawling slowly down her hairline.

Then she asked him, "Is this 11 or 11A?"

He knew exactly what to say. He was an expert in this. "11!" he said with authority. "See? Just look directly under the negative," he said, trying to make eye contact.

Usually, the subjects of her duplicates was nature. She'd traveled all over. She loved mountains and lakes. Her photographs were peaceful. She enlarged them to 8 by 10's sometimes, but usually she just ordered "dupes."

When he developed her roll, he handled them on the edges, with extra care. This time, there was a photo that really flipped him out. She was in the water, wearing a hat, smiling into the camera. Only there was a red swirly thing over the image. He studied the photo a long time before he figured out the red line was the string holding the camera lens cap to the camera that got in the way. Behind the red was her body, stark naked. He wondered who took the picture. Maybe she set the camera up herself and jumped into the water. It was hard to see much, so he covered the string parts with the smallest size Post-its. That way, he could imagine the whole outline of her, round breasts floating above the surface like small buoyant cantaloupes. Below the surface of the water - only a vague darkness. Just as he was adjusting the last Post-it and her shape emerged, his manager came over and looked over his shoulder.

"You've got a customer, I'll finish those," his manager said to him, grinning. He stripped off each Post-it, one by one, and stuck them to the plastic lining inside the wastebasket. He thought he'd kill the Man someday for that.

VI

He carefully tore off her receipt, making sure each perforation was exactly divided from the envelope, taking his time. She was watching him closely. Was it impatience she was feeling or was she admiring the size and shape of his hands? He was sure she could see them shaking. He hoped she'd notice and ask him if he was all right, if maybe he was ill or in need of help. Maybe she'd invite him over for coffee. She'd be sitting on a red velvet settee, fat brocade pillows propped up behind her, the kind of pillows with little mirrors in them. Her strong running legs would be tucked up underneath. She'd be in flowered tights and a long shirt unbuttoned to the middle of her sternum that would show off her flesh when she leaned over. She wouldn't take her eyes off him as she reached over to take his hand in hers. She would lead him into the light.

"Thanks," she said. She stuffed the receipt in the pocket of her shorts and bolted out the door. He knew by her address that she lived just a few blocks away. She must have been in a hurry to get home. Did she have someone waiting?

VII

She unleashed her dogs from the tree, patted their heads and said "Good boys and girls!" even though there was only one of each. She hadn't figured out how to address them except as "children" or "boys and girls." "Good boy and girl" sounded awkward and "dogs" was distancing. Calling them by name worked, but she needed a variant from time to time, so it was "boys and girls" since they were innocent like children are supposed to be. She loved her dogs. They were better than children or adults. They only required love.

Along the railroad tracks, goldenrod, blue asters and sumac hinted at fall. Things were changing. She was feeling nostalgic, smelling the misty rain that in a few weeks would be snow. It was okay to be alone. No children or husband was fine with her. She decided she was happy.

At home, she peeled onions and zucchini and garlic and carrots and threw them all into the Cuisinart. Hot soup would be delicious with rye bread. Everything was perfect.

VIII

He pulled up to the Quick Mart and parked half in the handicapped spot and half in the other. He didn't like getting car-door chips on his vehicle. It was a midnight blue Cadillac hearse with velvet curtains on the sides and fins in back. He needed a Pepsi and some Luckies. He was the only one he knew who still smoked Luckies. He was the only one he knew who did a lot of things. A doobie and a Lucky with a Pepsi and a Twix. That would do it. Oh, yes, and tonight he needed a couple of Coors, too.

Back in his basement apartment, he changed out of his work clothes and hung them up carefully. They reeked of emulsion. His temples throbbed. Maybe if he got his landlady to tie the necktie into a loop, with the ends just right, he could put it on and take it back off without the hassle. But, no, he could ask her about her garden and how it grew. He needed to keep her at arm's length. It was safer that way.

He checked under his pillow for the tools he needed. He wanted to get in. That was all he wanted, just to get in. Getting in meant everything. She would take care of him. He would give her gifts of food and flowers.

He would tell her about what it had been like, how he'd quit high school and gotten in with some bad people. He wouldn't have to use the word gang. That would frighten her. She had to be a college graduate, the way she moved and talked - like she knew by heart things he could never know. So he had to be careful or she'd call the cops or try to run away. He thought about the kind of environment that could contain her spirit - it would have to be full of space, yet secure.

So, he'd offer to fix her something to eat, like a cheese sandwich. Maybe he could even bring her a little package. With a red ribbon. Red was just right for her. She was so, well, vivid.

IX

She remembered rose petals under her feet, soft and silky. Running, running through the rose garden, her small feet slid across yellow and white and red rose petals that had fallen to the grass. A bronze fountain spewed water from cupids' mouths. They held their tiny penises with casual indifference. A female goddess like Botticelli's Venus stood in the center, barely covering her private regions with a sheer veil. The bronze figures weren't self-conscious, so neither was she. She took off her sandals, her shorts and halter top, and dipped her feet into the pool of water beneath the cascading fountains, cooling off, sharing relief with the gods. Clouds rose up in bundles of white, like dreams, like birth.

X

She exploded out of the dream like a shot and sat up in bed. 2 a.m. in digital red on her alarm clock. She threw off her nightgown in a night sweat. The male dog lay curled like a fawn at the foot of her bed. The female was snoring on the landing. If there were anything wrong, they would rise from slumber and seek its source. She would bark an alarm and he would lunge. They would do so from a history primitive and basic, one that kept her safe. Wouldn't they? Or were they getting too old and unreliable, used to reliable patterns. Had she remembered to turn on the security system? She wished she weren't so careless. It was a big townhouse and sometimes she heard noises at night. Was that a door that closed softly?

XI

He stood over her. She stared at the bulge in his pants. This intruder could be tamed. It had been two years since her self -defense class. Knees and nuts. Kick. Fight. Don't give in.

She sat up, gripping the covers. The female barked and barked and barked and finally grunted and lay back down. The male dog growled and bared his teeth.

"Hand me my nightgown," she said. He reached over on the floor for her nightgown. He looked like he might cry as he touched its lacy pink flowers. He turned it right side out and flapped it in the air to get the wrinkles out. He handed it to her by the straps, turning his face away while she slipped it over her head. How did he get in? Past the security system. Past the dogs. Past her dreams and nightmares. All these years, she'd been listening, alert, to the sounds of the night, the whir of the furnace, the scratching of oak limbs against the windows, an occasional siren in the distance. She now realized she was slumbering by day. Had he been there all along? Behind the curtain? In the closet? Under the bed?

XII

He sat on the bed, cross-legged, talking to her. He even brought popcorn, her favorite. It smelled of butter and salt, the way she liked it. She didn't lean over to take some, afraid to get close to him. But, he didn't make it look good, dipping his long fingers into it, and licking them one by one. His forearms were veiny, the kind that could crush her in an instant. The dog lay down, watching, poised to pounce.

His stories didn't connect. He told her all about his childhood, how he ran away from home, slept in alleys, panhandled for food. He was one of those guys on the street she turned her eyes from, but now his cornflower blue eyes held her captive. He talked about not being able to get the books he liked from the prison library and how he could never get his tie right on the job. She found herself lost in his long, loose hair, streaming around his shoulders like melted chocolate. It surprised her because it was so shiny and clean. She liked clean men—men with trim bodies and cropped hair, "suits" who were a little bit rugged. The way he described things—like it was all a game whose rules he didn't know —made him vulnerable, innocent.

XIII

He felt soothed, lulled into a trance by his own words. At last someone was listening to him. Someone who cared. Someone who understood. He told her everything - even about masturbating with the extra print he made of her in the nude. He thought she'd be angry, but instead she looked at him with eyes fixed on him, as if he mattered. Maybe she felt something for him. No one ever made him feel like that. She was quiet as stone, listening.

XIV

For just an instant, when she looked at him, looked deeply into his soul, so deeply it hurt his heart, he convinced himself she was the one.

But, he believed he understood her expressions. He had seen her eyes light up whitehot when she was happy and flatten to gray when she was sad. She turned her head away. She was crying. He was beginning to understand. She wanted him to leave, but couldn't say it. They had known each other a long time, in dreams at night when wild things stalk. He had known her as the prey and she knew him as predator.

He thought of his mother, of the world outdoors, of objects in his apartment that satisfied his cravings. He felt an urgency to go back to sift through the rubble from bombings that burned his flesh. Looking at her there, wrapped up and frightened, so vulnerable, made his body ache with fear and longing. Old wounds broke open. He needed to lick them in private.

XV

He got up off the bed, turned his back on her and walked out of the room. The dogs followed, sniffing and growling at his heels. The female nipped his thigh, close to his balls.

The male snagged his Achilles tendon. She rose from her bed to lock the doors behind him.

She'd know better next time. The signs were clear now. Even asleep she'd sense his presence, long before he came into view.

All He Saw Was Summer

Watching them makes me feel like an intruder, leering at something intimate behind lace curtains, but I can't help myself. I feel an upsurge of belief again, a regeneration of my spirit, which, if you must know, has sagged a little with age. They are the image of fresh love, the kind that unrolls its crenellations, undressed to its core. They prove that love is still in style, that it continues to be kind despite the coldness of virtual reality.

They glow like love stars in a constellation, impenetrable, distant: he, leaning in slightly, she, head bowed demurely toward him. Both somewhat shy, about the same height, ash-blond, big-eyed, and certain in their geometry. When they sit together, their shoulders, their thighs, their calves, their fingertips melt into a seamless stream. Their lips murmur indistinct secrets. I am both fascinated and embarrassed.

When they walk through the halls, their voices are low, quiet, blending into the raucous chaos surrounding them. They flow in and out, scarcely visible, two abreast, among a rush of bodies hurrying to class, shielded by the armor of love. By virtue of their existence, all witnesses are a bit sweeter, elevated by their gentle smiles.

I didn't notice Alex much during first semester among eighteen senior boys. He was a clown. I took his grinning to be smug, even sarcastic. His work, however, showed a serious side, a mature mind.

Now, second semester, his grin is actual happiness, a quality absent in most teenagers. His joy is rooted in a woman, a full-lipped, cow-eyed, lovely, long-legged girl. Alex and Liv aren't, at first blush, a likely match. She moved here from Germany because her father landed a corporate job in the city. He is Jewish, his grandfather a Holocaust survivor living in New York.

I expected my friends to be jealous, but they're totally cool when I tell them I can't hang out because I want to be with Alex. When I first came from Munich, I had no friends. Then I made the basketball team. One of my teammates has a brother who attended every game. I could feel him watching me when I dribbled and passed. When I scored, I could see him out of the corner of my eye flashing a huge smile. His mouth is large and takes up a third of his face. His eyes laugh too. Some guys laugh and their eyes are hard. At first I thought he looked a bit quatschkopf (crazy in the head). When he came down to the court with his parents right after a game and introduced himself, I already knew who he was but pretended like it was a surprise. I knew his name. I knew he was a break dancer. I knew he liked me.

From that moment, things between us moved fast. In Germany, we went to clubs in groups and had a lot of freedom. Parents here have to know everything. I'm really glad my parents don't ask a lot of questions. I wouldn't be comfortable telling them about our private times. I haven't loved anyone before. I guess I've been practicing for Alex. He takes me into his arms as if I were meant to exist there, like that's my place. It's funny, we come from completely different backgrounds, but we're alike. He finishes my sentences, putting two long fingers to my lips and whispering exactly what I mean to say before I have a chance to talk. Some people think it's not a good thing, that he doesn't let me speak, but that's not it. He speaks truth to me. When we're together alone, he kneels over me and talks to me and kisses me everywhere, tells me how I make him feel warm inside, like he's at home in a peaceful place. I love the things he says to me. I love the way he talks. He's funny and sweet and good.

Day after day, the two lovers come to class early to help me move chairs into a circle, throwing down their two cumbersome backpacks into a canvas heap, a mound of mutuality, between two chairs they claim next to me. One goes to the library, the other asks to go too. One turns in a poem or a paper, the other turns in a poem or paper just after. They work together like Leo and Anna Tolstoi. It's mutually productive, so I have no objection. If I believed one was doing the other's work, I would put a halt to it, but I know Alex's work, and it's very different from hers. They work independently together. The rest of the class, already accepted into college, and well into second-semester senioritis, act like they're doing me a favor to turn in assignments. Alex and Liv are not only prompt with their work, they're precise, even perfectionistic, rewriting and rewriting until it meets standards of A.

We're studying "Ode on a Grecian Urn" in class. It's about how fast life goes, and how these chicks are parading through a little village, which shows on the Grecian urn, or vaselike thing, and there are these pipes and boughs and heifer cows and the cows represent the young maidens who are "overwrought" and there are musicians playing songs and people who really like underdig the parade but feel sorta depressed because they know the time will be gone soon like a memory and it's all very cool and written in rhyme which we studied. The beat goes deep, you know? One chick is "unravish'd" which means she's still a virgin and they haven't had their "bliss," which means, well, it's obvious, but it's still beautiful because they're stuck there in this permanent waiting. Anticipating. This Keats guy is awesome, the way he writes about young love, so I think I'll try to write something for Livvy to show her how much I love her and tell her that we aren't going to be dead for a long time so let's be beautiful the way we love each other now. Let's take it and run. It's not like she doesn't want it and it's all about me, though. We only get together when it feels right, when we both want it. The word I have for it is bliss. That word is so cool. So I write an assigned poem that's supposed to be about the transience of life, but it's really written for Liv, and Ms. Gregory reads it aloud in class. Liv gets all red in the face and I think she's mad, but she's really happy. And proud. At least that's what she says. Being so close the way we are, it's easy to feel exactly how she's feeling most of the time. I hear her breathing in my own chest. I don't know which heartbeat is hers and which is mine. Then my beat speeds up, setting me on fire. I'm going to burst right out of my skin, but her soft look slows me way down. She has this way about her of looking at me like she's going to burn holes right through my face if I don't settle down, so I take my time and it's worth it. It's really worth it. She's changing me. I swear.

Dear Ms. Gregory,

I am writing to express my profound gratitude to you for inspiring our son, Alex. I've never seen him so happy. He can't wait to get to school. He talks about your class all the time. You have inspired in him something we've never seen. It wouldn't surprise me if he becomes a writer, thanks to you. I hope someday he'll write our family history. For now, though, he feels good about himself and his work. Whatever it is you're doing in class, we are deeply grateful to you. I am sending a copy of this letter to the Headmaster and Chair of the English department.

Sincerely,

Herbert Westerman, M.D.

Of course, this is every teacher's answered prayer, a parent who not only likes writers and sends you a fan letter but also sends a copy of the letter to your boss. The truth is I think the boy has talent. Natural rhythm. He writes almost perfect iambic pentameter without forcing it. Rhymed poetry isn't fashionable, but so what? In class, we discuss how quickly youth is gone, how transient the "spring," how beautiful the "heifer's...silken flanks with garlands drest." I teach them to scan for meter and rhyme. For me, it's a blackboard exercise, performed year after year, abab, etc., a study of the common themes of literature: love, death, war...and they teach me over and over that "beauty is truth, truth beauty," "that is all/Ye know on earth, and all ye need to know." They rekindle in me the reminder that Keatsian love did exist in my life once, "unravished," "happy, happy..."

Alex and Liv coo at each other like they're part of the pastoral parade, "piping songs forever new," marching around the Grecian urn. I feel nostalgic and, yes, a bit melancholic. I admire the hell out of what they have and am maybe a little jealous of their youth and innocence. They know the truth of beauty and the beauty of truth. They are experiencing it on the inside track. Their poetry is equally poignant, well-crafted, and sensitive to Keatsian themes. Others in the class are either jaded from being jilted or wary from disbelief that joy can exist in today's world. Others suspend their disbelief and take Keats at his word, knowing in some instinctive way that their friends are the real deal, well, about as real as it gets at eighteen.

In his last couplet of a sixteen-line poem, Alex writes, "Once bonded together but now unstrung/At last we live! Forever young." And she writes, "Within each child a glim'ring light/A soul that's silver and pure/A beauty that lives and can't be changed/A treasure no one can immure."

Both of them finish the final project—to create a large book, a composite of all their writings, in an artistic form— thoroughly and creatively. They drive one another to achieve great things, not just good things, but truly lovely. She turns in hers first, with a beautifully constructed, color-coded table of contents, each section decorated according to what it is— essays, poems, short stories, journal entries. His comes in second, not quite as colorful, but well organized, clean, and complete. Books from the rest of the class trickle in all week, fragmented, halfhearted—a disappointment. One student has the audacity to say he wasn't told he had to keep his writings and has thrown his work away. I've had it on their assignment sheets for weeks.

Alex and Liv sustain me, my icons of scholarship and true love.

Then one day, I'm late and I'm distracted. The air smells old and chalky as a blackboard gone unwashed for years. I look around. The lovers are here, but instead of next to each other, they sit within the ranks of gender. In high school, boys often sit with each other as a kind of protective barrier against girls, potential heartbreakers, more at ease with each other anyway. I have come to expect this. Alex and Liv are the sole exception.

But, today she is sitting in the middle of the girls, and he is sitting with the boys. My bearings are unhinged.

I search everyone's faces. Nothing. Surely they're acting. Someone will laugh or burst into tears. Yet no one says a word or signal of anything unusual. They seem to be saying, "We all knew it wouldn't last. Where've you been? Get over it and move on."

Don't they realize how important they are to the future of humanity? Alex and Liv prove sensitivity still exists in this callous world. How could they split without letting me in on it? They've robbed me of my musings.

Suddenly I am immensely lonely. I've been a fool. What makes me think that I know jack about teenage love? It's been decades. Let's face it. Things change. I'm older now. Young lovers don't operate like they used to. It's just sport.

Besides, I'm their teacher, not their choreographer. I'm there to inspire them to academic heights, not get involved in their personal lives. I plunge to earth with a thud. How dull. How mortal. How unsightly.

This cruel joke lasts throughout the period. My imagination muses:

A month or two, hot and heavy—total obsession—and then it's over? So what happened? Lover's quarrel? Her father grounded her? His grandfather told him it was an insult to his heritage? She had to get an abortion? Her mother said she had to free herself up because of college? One of them found someone else on a whim? She's returning to Germany? Everything has a beginning and an ending.

At lunch, I tell my colleague and good friend, Snappy.

"Get over it," she says. "You know it's a fantasy. Why are you involved? What's that about? Why do you care?"

"I'll tell you why I care," I say. "Day after day, year after year, pimply, angst-ridden teenagers stuff their awkward bodies under too-small desks and earnestly try to learn from me, despite hormonal longings, ennui, and Facebook. In turn, they entertain me, they enlighten me, and they enlarge me. I owe it to them and to myself to care just a little if one or two of them suffers the fallout of an exploded dream."

"You could get more entertainment from Netflix, more enlightenment from reading O magazine, and more enlargement from a carton of ice cream."

"Not the same. None of those things gets me out of bed in the morning. Each one of these kids is a little miracle. Don't you remember when you lost yourself in someone else?" I say.

"No. Can't say as I've ever lost myself. What a frightening concept. I don't even think it's healthy. I like being me. Separate from anyone."

"Remember in the song 'Hello, young lovers,' there's a line about 'when the earth smells of summer'? It's like being born, drinking in the world…" I say, dreamily.

"Oy vay."

Later that day, I think back to three years ago, when Snappy first described this job. We were swimming at sunrise. We locked our bikes by the lifeguard stand, threw off our cover-ups and flip-flops, and put on goggles. It had just rained. The lake was deliciously cold, grey, and calm.

"Just a few classes, Gregs, it'll be great for you!" she said. She was right. The money is good for my husband and me, who, like the rest of the country's retirees, are stretched financially.

When I retired several years ago, it was exhilarating at the time—like jumping into a cold lake, swift and shocking. The water filled my ears, nose, and mouth. Big decisions are like that. You go to the edge, look out at the water, say a little prayer, suck in the air around you, trying to exhale, and hurl yourself out into the lake. Hesitation is shocked out of you by the jolt and pressure of icy water bracing your limbs.

I took this new job, but forgot details like what malcontents say to each other on Fridays: "TGIF!" i.e., every day is torture until the weekend. I forgot the faculty lounge gossip about students who don't conform to the norm. I forgot about parental pressure for performance, glassy-eyed students who'd rather be home sending obscene photos of themselves to strangers online or running around outdoors with pretend guns in hot pursuit of each other in a grisly game called Assassins. I forgot about student stories of alcoholic parental beatings, pregnancies, self-injurious behavior, anorexia.

I secretly wonder, after taking the plunge, if I'm really teaching again to prove to myself that I can still do it. I find myself discussing issues as they come up that many other teachers rarely face: clitoridectomies, the pink-ification and cute-ification of American culture, interracial politics.

"I don't like pink because it's popular or girlie-girl. I just happen to like the color, okay?" says Rachelle, an African-American girl, fuchsia nail polish painted on artificial fingernails that curl around her raspberry pink Hello Kitty! backpack, which she draws closer to her feet. She blinks at me under rose-pink glittery eyelids.

"Pink looks really good on your cinnamon skin, Rachelle, but it might be totally racist to allow you to be an exception to the rule without at least mentioning what our culture does. The fact is your conformity compromises you."

"I don't know whatchyoo talkin' 'bout, but I jes' like wearin' pink. 'Sides, it's really none of your business."

Midday, I get sleepy, heavy-lidded, head-nodding sleepy. Unless I jazz it up a little, it's routine. I've done it all, had every type of conversation with teenagers and their doting or negligent parents.

And then along came Liv and Alex to wake me up.

"Who are these coming to the sacrifice? To what green altar, O mysterious priest…"

It's Friday before prom. Right on schedule, snowy-white apple blossoms are at their height in my side yard. They fill the yard with graceful petals bursting through buds, popping open in multiples, flowering and full of birds. Last week, I picked up two Bohemian waxwings from my deck, their soft bodies perfect, their tiny beaks crushed from flying excitedly into the windows, mistaking the images they see reflected back as their own true loves. Each one—drunk as

Narcissus, suddenly dead, its delicate yellow breast no longer beating, its belly full from a surfeit of fruit—fits exactly into a pint-sized Ziploc baggie. I bury several of them every year.

Liv comes in early as always. She is puffy-eyed and red-faced.

I can't resist anymore. "Liv, you don't have to answer this, but, well, I just wondered, are you and Alex still an item?"

"Item?"

"Yes, are you boyfriend and girlfriend?"

Liv smiles. The color of her eyes intensifies from blue to turquoise. Her cheeks redden. "Yes," she says, "we are."

"Oh, because I thought since yesterday you weren't sitting together and since it looked like you'd been crying, maybe…"

"Oh, that's funny. The air is funky with pollen this spring and I'm allergic. We just took different seats, that's all."

"Oh, well, I was just wondering." I feel stupid nosing around in their lives. Am I a voyeur? A pedophile? More students file in.

Later, at lunchtime, I check in with Snappy, my armchair psychotherapist.

"What have you got invested in this, Gregs?" she asks.

"I believe they know something I don't. In fact, I wonder if I've missed it altogether."

"Missed what?"

"I don't know. That's just it. They were doing so well with Keats. They knew the language of love. They got it."

"C'mon, Gregs, Keats was just a kid when he died. He didn't know nearly as much as you and I do, now that we're, well...seniors."

"Right. Keats was orgasmic about spring, and we've lived and loved in every season, all the way through winter and back again to spring."

"Exactly. Cut yourself some slack."

"You mean the one who counts is the one that sticks around after the parade? Listens to the piping in your heart and dances in the glittering prisms that radiate light from snow that reflects off the crown of your head?"

Snappy rolls her eyes.

Monday, Liv comes, weaving a little, into my room under the weight of her backpack and burdens, cheeks smeared with mascara, breath rushing out in little pulsating sobs.

"Liv, what happened?" I say.

"Oh, Ms. Gregory. We broke up!" One loud wail, a hiccup, and she is silent.

"I am so sorry..." I begin.

Liv tells her story in a trembling voice.

When she's finished, I launch into a speech, partly to keep her from sobbing, partly because I think I know what to say. "Liv, Keats died at twenty-five. He and his urn were stuck in summer, arrested in time. Keats was too young to know the joy of all seasons. Do you see? 'Forever young' is death."

She looks at me as if I'm the one who's quatschkopf. "Ms. Gregory, it's okay, really. It's not about Keats. Alex said he'd changed because of me. He didn't. He couldn't. Maybe it lasted as long as it was meant to. Alex meant every word he said."

"At least at the time," I say.

"Every word," she repeats.

Stories from Old Pines

I. SPORT

A gigantic black lab puppy wearing a metal-pronged choke collar bounded from his yard and circled round me. I knew from earlier encounters that Sport was more brawn than brains, and this time I was on Rollerblades.

I came to a screeching halt when my neighbor, John, appeared and beckoned me to approach, a feat I found tricky to perform on an incline in loose gravel and sand with a wild dog off leash.

"Hi!" I said. "How are you?" I was still upright.

"Oh, pretty darned good, but the stress is terrible."

"It is? I'm so sorry!" Sport was sniffing the hindquarters of our ever-so-feminine Beardie, Calliope, who was also off-leash but relatively calm.

"Yes, I have to paint this mailbox post here, go to the Laundromat, pick up a thing or two at the grocery store, and come back for the wife to go out to eat at Foxy's. I don't know if I can do it all." He placed his hands on what was intended to be his waist and stretched backward, belly swelling out between red suspenders. Torn jeans and a paint-splotched T-shirt seemed an appropriate outfit for today's chores.

"That doesn't sound too stressful," I said. He laughed, his face melting into soft puddles.

"Oh, you're easy," he said, making me laugh. "Get over here!" he shouted at the dog. Sport was still circling and Calliope was repeatedly sitting down and running away, tail between her legs.

"I don't mind your dog. I just don't want to get between our two dogs. I might fall. Where's Foxy's?"

"Foxy's? In Spooner. Get over here, Sport! What's your dog's name again?"

"Her name's Calliope. Is the food any good?" I said.

"Oh, terrific, we like it a lot. Beer's good. Drinks are cheap."

"And the food?" I asked again.

"Shrimp's terrific."

"Is it grilled?"

"No, fried. Calliope, huh? Like a merry-go-round?"

"Exactly. Also the muse of poetry. How do you get to Foxy's?" I asked.

"Aw, it's easy to find when you know the way. You take the first left after you see the sign for Spooner. You follow that road about a quarter mile, and take the second right and then a left by the school, and you go down the big hill that just kinda ends up by the railroad tracks. You'll see a crossing sign and you cross there at the tracks. Then, you'll see a dingy ole brown house. Turn left onto the dirt road that looks like it's not going to be a road at all. But it is and you take it until you can't go any further. You'll see a sign that says Foxy's, but that isn't your turn. That's just a sign to let you know you're on the right road."

"Tricky," I said.

"Well, some folks'll get confused here. Keep going straight another mile or so, go down another hill, and then there's a split rail fence on your left... Sport! I told you, now!" Sport was lifting a leg on a pine tree while Calliope was sitting as close to me as she could without tripping me up.

"You know, I think I'd probably call Foxy's for directions. I'll never remember all that."

"You want an easier way? Cut right through town. It's longer, but you hang a left by the DQ and then go about five blocks until you get to the third stop sign. You hang a right and then another left and then go about three miles until you see an old barn with a coupla brown-spotted cows in the pasture. Guernseys."

"Okay..."

"You follow right off the fork in the road until you see a billboard advertising the casino down in Turtle Lake."

"Mm-hmm."

"Keep going until you see a big pasture with a hand-painted sign for Surrey bulls. You're out of milking territory and into ranching country over there, y'see."

"Yup." Sport's circles were getting tighter as he was brushing dangerously closely to my leg. Calliope was hiding behind me.

"Go on," I said.

"Then you'll come to a turkey hunting registration and pass the little cemetery on the hill there and pretty soon you hit Sand Lake."

"Sand Lake?"

"Yup. You're gettin' close now. You'll pass Simpson's

boat storage. There's a big eagle's nest up in the telephone pole. You'll miss it unless you know what you're lookin' for." He looked me dead in the eye. "Been there for years. They just keep making it bigger and bigger."

"And Sand Lake? How do I know when I've come to Sand Lake?"

"There's a little sign that you can barely see unless you're really looking for it.

At night you won't see it at all."

"So I guess if you set out early enough, the sun will still be up."

"Ha! Right you are. Well, as a matter of fact, cloudy and rainy days are kinda hard too because Foxy's is set way down in the grass like a prairie chicken."

"You know. When we're at the cabin, we eat at home most of the time. Are there other lakes you pass?"

"Just a couple more. Bass Lake and Round Lake."

"Yah, well, maybe sometime…" I rolled back on my blades to turn around.

He interrupted me. Sport had returned to sniff around Calliope's back. "Sport? What did I tell you? I mean it now!" Sport put his big head down between his front legs and dropped to the road next to Calliope.

I started to roll backward by way of saying goodbye. "Well, thanks for the tip."

"Okay, then, see ya. Say hi to the mister. Sorry Sport doesn't mind his manners around your carousel."

II. OLYMPIAD

It seems like a lot of guys around here are named John. But this John is taller and mightier than the rest. He's even a doctor. And aren't doctors the closest we mortals get to gods? I am amazed at his stamina, his lean physique, his results! He stands well over 6'6". His teeth are even and white, his skin the leathery brown that suggests virility on men past a certain age—men whose skin has achieved the texture of worn hide that's been around the horn.

I wouldn't have encountered this John if I hadn't secretly explored his garden tucked away off the private road, scarcely visible. Most yards in lake country are simply marked by fading headless loon mailboxes, toilet bowls filled with volunteer grasses and milkweed; battered milk cans; or fields of daisies that last until they're mowed under. John's garden, once discovered, is dazzling and inviting.

He has invited Calliope and me to stroll down the flower-strewn paths, to share in the glory of Gethsemane kissed by sunshine with no crucifixion to follow. Terraced down to the lake, his garden is a spectacular riot, each flower clamoring for attention.

He has outdone everyone near and far, throughout every county from our lake home in Wisconsin down to Minneapolis. His clearing is filled with yellow, pink, and white Asiatic lilies; variegated hostas; wild roses; purple and yellow irises; white marigolds, ferns, and sunflowers—all spilling over one another in a plethora of abundant color. His flowers have a way of surprising you at each curve that slopes down to Crane Lake.

A bed of dahlias greets you by the shuffleboard court; sweet little tricycles and old red wagons filled with impatiens and vinca decorate the greens; hand-painted rocks monogrammed by grandchildren nestle down amongst the flowers. He is not only a gardener extraordinaire, but he also has some kind of magical superpower that keeps animals at bay. His sprinkler system must have a motion detector to fend off foraging deer.

John's garden didn't happen by accident. There was a tornado here in 2002 that leveled many yards, taking scores of native white pine. Instead of bemoaning the loss, he arranged to have truckloads of manure deposited on his rubble. And he began to plant. Every time I see him, he's bending over, weeding, spreading mulch, or planting new beds of flowers. John seems driven by sheer love of soil, watching it spring to life as he nurses young plants and flowers to their ripest conclusion. When he works, his knees are married to the earth. His hands are invisible to the wrists. He is a titan of terrain.

To transport the dozens of flats of flowers, he drives a luxury SUV with a huge cargo space from which I've seen him unload dozens of bags of mulch and crate after crate of dazzling flowers, all in the midst of a deep green virgin pine forest.

DNR pamphlets would disapprove of the non-native species John has introduced, to say nothing of the fertilizer and other types of additives he uses to maintain this amazement. The DNR would further specify that John's garden may encroach on the proper number of feet from shore a garden should be. But herein lies the conundrum, perhaps his tragic flaw. Can John be a true Olympiad if he defies laws, singlehandedly building a monument to pure aesthetics despite its effects on the environment? Is this, after all, what the Greeks had in mind when they prayed to Zeus—that he was infallible and had a superhuman ego?

I have no answer to that, not being a scholar of Greek myth. I can tell you, I both admire John's garden and wonder about the nutrients that may leech into the soil from flats of flowers grown in greenhouses somewhere, grass, fertilizer, and mulch so close to a wilderness lake.

Once John took pity on me—an unabashed admirer, doubtless one amidst a throng—and offered discarded fern that he had thinned. I was grateful and planted them in our garden, knowing they are native to our forest.

Along with the enormous scale of his investment and formal beauty is the scale of his expenditure. It has taken a sprinkler system and a gargantuan amount of plant material to create and maintain such splendor. However, if medals were being distributed for the finest garden this side of the St. Croix Valley, he deserves the gold.

A few years ago, Marshall and I ran into him and his wife, Hera, at a funeral gathering. "What are you doing here?" she asked in an icy tone. Apparently surprised at her own bluntness, she modified her question, "That is, how do you know…?"

"Well, she (the deceased) was a dear friend of our son's," I answered. Hera's eyes widened and she smiled politely, patting her very large, paisley scarf, one end tossed casually but carefully over her square shoulder, before she turned to continue socializing with her familiars.

Not too long after that, after one of my strolls through his garden, I invited the two of them with their children and grandchildren over to our lake home on the adjoining lake. They came. They and their children and the heirs apparent ate our fresh poppy seed banana cake with warm fruit and real whipping cream. And we even found a few things we had in common.

However, one day Marshall and I parked our car close by and were getting Calliope leashed up to take our usual stroll around the loop road past John's house. From the direction of town came a tall, gaunt man and a young boy, both on bicycles. As soon as they approached, I could see it was Gardener John. Not seeming to recognize us, he cocked his head and spoke sharply to us as if we were fallen from grace and needed to be quickly removed from Olympus, "Out of gas?!"

"What's that?" Marshall said, smiling, not yet comprehending that John didn't seem to know us.

"Are you out of gas?" he repeated loudly.

"No, no, we always park here and walk," Marshall explained.

"Thanks anyway," I said.

John's eager expression paled. He had wanted to perform an heroic deed exhibiting his godly beneficence as an example to his grandson, but we weren't cooperating. He sped past us without further comment toward his home, spitting up gravel behind him.

John may be mortal, demigod, or god, who achieves success and floats slightly above ground, levitating without support. If he knew you once, there is no guarantee he'll know you the next time. He exists in a kind of superstratum, a vaporless vacuum of impermeability. Eyes on the prize or, in this case, the flowers.

I don't visit his garden much anymore. I'd rather watch the rusty needles fall thickly from the majestic pine trees in our yard. They seem so effortless and beautiful in an ordinary sort of way.

III. LESTER

I pull into the dark garage, the heady smell of pine flooding my senses. I am breathing deeply again after a particularly hectic week in the city, already imagining myself swimming in our magnificent lake, arm over arm, not another soul in sight. I feel my cares melting away when I have nothing to do but scan the horizon for the tallest pine, my marker that it's time to turn around and swim back toward home shore.

I unfold out of the car after our long ride, lift the back gate, and out springs Calliope, my sweet merry-go-round, running and barking through a thick bed of pine needles, searching out a spot to anoint.

A loud gunshot bursts through the woods, puncturing my fantasy, jolting me into the moment. Calliope gallops back to me, quivering.

The shots are coming from the woods, I mutter aloud, stepping hesitantly out of the car door, trying to peer through the trees. In each hand, I carry groceries and odds and ends from the car into the cabin.

Lester will know. I'll call him for an answer. He keeps up with everything. Because he's the only one around,

Lester's the go-to guy for information. He knows how long the baby loon has been on the lake and what day the sandhill cranes depart.

Lester flies two flags on his property—one a Confederate flag, and the other a Marine Corps flag. The only year-round resident, his little white cottage is directly across from us on our small, remote lake. Between us is the deepest, cleanest, prettiest part of the lake. Not a tendril of a weed.

"Hi, Violet," I begin. "How are you?" Violet, Lester's wife, has a bad heart and has been dwindling for years.

"I'm better, thanks. How are you?"

"You know, I'm really fine except I heard a shot. Sounded like it was right next door. Doesn't hunting season begin on Thanksgiving?"

"Hang on a minute." There's a loud clunk as Vi puts the phone down.

Vi picks up the receiver again. "Yup. Handgun's missin'. I think he's out shootin' in the trees."

"In the trees? Why?"

"Oh, there's a branch he can't get down. He keeps shootin' at it, hoping he'll scare it down." She laughs a husky, smoke-filled laugh and lapses into spasmodic coughing.

"Hmm," I say.

We often hear shooting when Lester and Vi's son and grandson visit from Tennessee. Their shots vary from the popping of handguns and the pinging of rifles to the rat-a-tat-tat of semiautomatics. The deafening reverberations might as well be in our front yard. With little to do but watch television, smoke, and watch his wife linger, this ex-Marine is someone I may need in a pinch, so I limit my comments about their intense and persistent gunfire. If I call to request a temporary halt, he usually cooperates.

I hear some explanatory conversation in the background whereupon Lester takes the phone from Violet. "'Lo." he says, "Wife says you don't like the shootin.' They're just practicin' their huntin'. Don't like to say too much since Junior only comes once in a while, but I'll tell him to quit for now if it's bothering you," he says.

"Thank you, Lester, very much," I say. "I really appreciate it."

I take a swim, hoping they'll hold off long enough for me to get out of the water. *I wonder what the loons feel in the water from the gunfire.* When I swim across the lake, I don't swim all the way to Lester's dock. Although I have no proof, I believe he has binoculars trained on me. I swim directly toward his house and then stop at my white pine stretching way above the tops of the others, where I turn around, and swim back. Calliope attends at the end of the dock, paws crossed, scanning the woods, then watching me, then the woods.

As I'm getting dressed, I find myself thinking about Lester looking in the windows. He's only done it once, to my knowledge, but I have to admit that one time made me uneasy.

About three years ago, I was standing in the kitchen, fully clothed, thank God. Suddenly, I saw a red hat pass by just under the window frame. Kind of bouncing up and down in a half-marching, half-limping gait. Lester.

I burst through the front door, the screen door slamming loudly behind me.

"Lester," I said in my most assertive voice, "can I help you?"

"Just checkin' on things," he said. "Thought I saw smoke across the lake and since there was a fire here once, I wanted to make sure everything was all right."

"I'm burning some brush," I said, my mind trying to fathom why he didn't call first. Or better yet, why didn't he come to the door and ring the bell?

It's scary sometimes at night here alone. I stash a row of defense weaponry on top of my bedcovers—a rosewood truncheon, my cell phone, and our cordless land line. We have installed a blind over the outside door that has a direct sightline to my bed. When I close my eyes, I dream I'm being hunted.

An Anniversary Story

This story begins one fine April morning, when the fragrance of delicate lilacs sliced the air, when limey, new oak leaves gently trembled against the window, and our dogs stretched their legs getting ready for their first walk of the day. I creaked open our front door to retrieve the morning paper and sensed a presence. Looking up, I spotted an unusual sight. Curled up under a juniper bush on the West side of our planter beds, high above the driveway, was a mama Mallard, staring up at me with small black eyes. Frozen to the front mat, I studied her situation, named her Mabel and shut the door. She arrived just two weeks from the time my husband Marshall and I were getting ready to depart for a trek in Italy.

When we were little, my sister received two pet ducks that grew and grew and ate the badminton net and the grass and pooped everywhere until they disappeared one day only to reappear on our dinner plates. Neither my sister nor I is fond of roast duck.

All morning, I mulled over Mabel's safety. Wouldn't the mail carrier walking up and down the steps disturb her? What about the traffic in and out of our front door? And what about the eight foot drop from the planter bed to the

concrete driveway below? Why didn't Mabel think of that? I googled Mallard and discovered Mabel's gestation period was 28 days, putting the birth of her ducklings right in the middle of Tuscany.

Meanwhile, we got used to each other. If I approached her too quickly or if it rained too hard, her wings rose, her feet dropped, and she was off the nest, headed straight through the sky, to an unknown destination. From a curled up gentle, docile bird, she morphed into a wild torpedo, gone with barely a flap. Each time this happened, I worried she wouldn't come back and blamed myself for not protecting her properly.

Six days later, she was joined by a friend, whom I named Mamie.

Daily, I reported the duck doings to Marshall, with whom I was about to celebrate our fortieth wedding anniversary. He took barely a passing interest. I suggested a ramp down the stairs to protect the two families of ducklings when they arrived. He grumbled, shook his head, and walked away, which often happens when I come up with an idea. He believes that if he ignores me long enough, I will give up. Since I have lots of ideas, he is right about half of the time. The other half of the time, I latch onto an idea and repeat it until I wear him down. As soon as he reaches that hang-dog, "I-give-up. Uncle!" expression, I pounce on him and drive it home.

Like regal queens on silken pillows, Mamie and Mabel surrounded themselves in a halo of tiny soft feathers tipped in white. I don't know if their hormones cause the down to naturally molt or if they pull their feathers out with their beaks, but the down successfully camouflages and warms the eggs when the mother is out for food or respite.

Our trip was a week away. I said, "Do we want to come home to innocent little ducks, smashed flat on the driveway? Or do we want to save them?" Quietly, and with a certain amount of resigned grumpiness, Marshall cleared out a path in the garage and brought out his table saw. Next, he measured the planters. Mabel and Mamie looked on. From our healthy stash of raw materials, long boards became ramps and planks. More measuring. On came Marshall's protective goggles. It got noisy.

Mabel flew away.

It poured rain. Marshall pulled his table saw in under the eaves. More buzzing. More measuring. Up went enclosures to prevent the ducklings from dropping to their deaths. Next came a system of walls and ramps for the ducklings' safe departure from their nests. Last came rubber mats to keep them from slipping as they waddled down toward the lake.

Neighbors stopped by to inquire and chuckle at the entire procedure. What they said in private I don't know. I put up a waterproof sign for the mail carrier and other visitors to respect the ducks' privacy and use the side door. Our front steps transformed into an elaborately constructed skyway system for a swift and dependable ducky departure to the lawn, and onward to the lake nearby. Mamie watched the whole thing serenely perched on her downy nest. Mabel was still gone. We were to leave the next day.

Our dog sitter, Brent, who works at the University of Minnesota Veterinary Hospital, supervised last minute touches. The night before we left, he reported hearing a clump-clumping up the ramp. That morning, Mabel was back on her nest.

We flew away, leaving Mabel and Mamie to Brent, along with a camera. There were no mallards in Tuscany, but when we came home, three weeks later, we ran to the front stairs. It smelled wild—duck birth wild. All the eggs but two had hatched.

Brent said, "I took photographs of Mabel's ducklings. Four little ones fell off the ramp and scrambled down the wrong way. I scooped them up in a box and plopped them down behind Mabel. Then I helped them march across the street to the lake. There were nine total. Mamie's eleven eggs cracked open six days later, but I didn't see it. Twenty in all."

I plucked feathers from the vines, removed the balls of down from the dirt, gently placed the unhatched eggs in the garbage, wondering, despite all known scientific fact, if they might come to life on their own. I planted my impatiens, and watered the whole area, recovering ownership.

2006, a year later, almost to the day, at lilac time, a drake and hen perched on our roof, claiming it. "Hey, all you flyby ducks. This pad is ours!" Mabel and her mate. Soon, she sat on her old nest. Six days later, Mamie arrived. How did Mabel and Mamie find us? Did they travel in the same flock? What made them think in the first place it was a good deal at our house? Are Mabel and Mamie smart or stupid? What about us?

Our house looks like a construction zone again, but we like to watch them roost and share them with the neighbors, and when they're finished, reclaim our planters and fluff up our junipers.

We remodeled the ramp system. It's a skyway and series of funnels and planks akin to an airport with runways. When he was making modifications, Mabel perched on the edge of the planter box as he spoke quietly to her, explaining his role in her life, and she waddled comfortably back to her spot. Years of experience using a table saw, a Master's Degree in Architecture, a lifetime of education as an architect and realtor have come to this.

If Mabel and Mamie return year after year, how will we ever move? What about their children and children's children? We have responsibility. The maze of mats, planks and hinges all over our front steps each spring, stored alongside the house in winter, make us odd ducks.

Are you wondering, what do these ducks have to do with our anniversary?

Upon reflection, I recognize it's no accident that Mamie and Mabel picked our home to roost. Marshall and I have reached a state of harmony that spawns nesting things. Three new grandchildren are proof. Additional proof is our recent reconnection with foreign exchange students whom we've hosted all our married life, from Serbia to Malaysia.

Rather than shoo away either Mabel or Mamie to spare the aesthetics of our front stairs, we made room. This is one key to a good marriage. To hell with appearances. Entertain the happy events that fly unexpectedly into your world. Watch them roost and when they're finished, let them go. Stay open for the next event.

Next, wait for your spouse to catch up to you if you're certain your idea is important. Don't assume she isn't listening. After a time, if it's right for both of you, it will happen.

Fourthly, respect your differences. Early in April, a Mallard drake stood in the middle of our street for several days for no apparent reason. I've heard of daddy drakes paddling around on people's roofs. Staking out territory takes many forms. Every drake is different. Every hen is different. Mabel and Mamie are very different from each other. Mabel was shy and frightened of thunder, staying under the bush until she would fly away for periods of time, sometimes overnight. Mabel sat in the open on her eggs, despite the weather, and never blinked an eye. They both made it to the lake.

Fifthly, there's a great deal of learning together. Not all my questions about the ducks were answered. When I told this story to a friend, she scoffed, "Wood ducks nest in trees. They must fall a long ways. Nothing happens to them. Ducklings have soft bones."

"But," I said, wood ducks have woods or water underneath them. Our Mallards would have had concrete."

Some of our neighbors tell me we're the buzz by the watercooler and at some dinner tables. I got to thinking about why that is. Marshall and I are a little "different", to use a Midwestern expression. It takes gumption to be different. Most folks don't build duck ramps. Most people's marriages don't last forty years either. And that's the point of this story.

Skateboards and a Sheepdog

Gus leaps three feet in the air, his open mouth appearing dangerously close to my face. "Out for a walk? I can't contain my joy!" he barks, leaping and leaping. A handsome sheepdog with long, silky hair and a bouncing, happy gait, his appearance attracts people immediately. Children tug at their parents' arms and point. A parent asks, "Excuse me. What kind of dog is that?" Prospective dog owners ask, "Does he require a lot of brushing?"

"Yes," I say. "He's a Bearded Collie. You're welcome to pet him. I'll hold him right here while you stand to his side and pet him." I crouch down to demonstrate, petting him and stroking his back from head to tail. "His name's Gus. Sit, Gus. We're a therapy team. I ought to groom him at least twice a week but I don't."

"Where's puppy's ears?" a little brown girl in a pink hat stops to ask, partly hiding behind her mother because Gus is twice her size.

"Here they are," I say, squatting down, weaving my fingers through the layers of his black-and-white coat, finding an ear and lifting it up gently. "You can pet him. He won't hurt you. Or you can scratch him right here." I scratch behind Gus's ear, flipping his ponytail back to show his eyes. The child giggles and reaches her small, chubby fingers out to touch his hair, then squeals and recoils.

"Look! He has a ponytail too!" says the girl's mother.

"That keeps the hair out of his eyes so we can make eye contact," I say.

Gus failed the therapy dog test twice because he jumped up on the tester in loving exuberance. When he learned to keep all four paws on the ground, he passed. On the job at senior residences and schools, he's so obedient, people remark how "chill" he is. I laugh to myself, knowing the many sides of Gus. This is my dream, to share joy with others so they'll feel like I do when I'm with him.

Today's the first day of full sun we've felt in Minneapolis since February. As soon as it hits fifty, flocks of people, nearly hysterical in their frenzy to conquer Lake Calhoun, burst out of their dwellings with ebullience, play volleyball in bikinis, and run headlong around the lake, earbuds or fitness devices draped across their half-naked bodies. Men in neon-green shoes with winter bellies chase visions of youth. Muslim women in long, bright skirts and hijabs flow gracefully in threesomes. Young couples in the bloom of romance rush the season in provocative, sheer clothing. Apple trees are aching to break their shells and burst into bloom. Orioles call in shrill melodies as they dip and flit elusively from one limey branch to another. Everyone has a role in the rites of spring.

It's Saturday afternoon, the busiest time to go for a walk with Gus. Bad choice. I hate steering through obnoxious cell phone conversations. It's an assault to my ears. Gus knows I mean business because I've put on his working harness and

scarf. He glances up at me every few minutes to forecast my intent. He can tell by the tension on the leash if I'm at all bothered. A typical herding dog, he senses trouble before it happens. When he gets carried away, trying to shepherd in all potential threats, I rein him in.

He trots along beside me, connected to his harness by a worn leather leash, drawn smart and taut. Gus makes the world friendly. Since I carry a small purse filled with baggies, treats, and Gus's business cards to be handed out for special admirers, I'm ready if anyone stops me. On the back side of his photograph card, a gift when we make therapy visits, I describe Gus as "athletic, agile, and witty." To make known his fallibility, I add, "Gus hates loud wheely things like Rollerblades and skateboards."

Several strings of rollerbladers fly by, the sound of their grinding wheels painful to Gus's sensibilities. When I see one coming toward us, I dig into my little bag and bring out small morsels of venison and sweet-potato kibble. He has learned to look up at my bag when a rollerblader approaches. My second bad choice is to walk in the same one-way direction as the people on wheels, so they are able to sneak up behind us before I can hear them. The fact that Gus is able to hear them before I do makes him jumpy. Gus tolerates rollerbladers better than skateboards.

A bearded, twenty-something man, wearing bright-green sunglasses that hide his eyes, wheels right up to us fast from behind on his skateboard, uncomfortably close, brushing against us, passing us on our path designated for walkers only. Gus leaps up and twists to growl and snap at him, this threat to our space.

I call out, "Hey, wrong path! Wheels on the upper path!"

The man shouts back, "What's wrong with your dog, lady? Can't you get him under control?" He hops off his board and holds it out from his body, under Gus's nose. Gus lunges at it, growling.

I stop short and yell. "You belong on the upper path! Wheels up there!" I point to the curving path a few yards up from the walking path. "My dog hates skateboards! It hurts his ears. Please. Move up there!"

A young threesome passes me and the skateboarder, turns to laugh at the scene. "That was craaazy! He's so cuuute!" says one girl, hair dyed black, arms and neck covered with tattoos of elaborate hearts, flowers, and a dagger dripping blood down her creamy shoulder. "That was wiiiild!" *Wild?* I think to myself. *They're confusing us with reality television. They have no idea how scary this is.* The other girl, plump and blond, in a black satin skirt, with a broad-chested, smiling guy, almost seven feet tall, complete the trio of spectators. They pause. Speechless, mouths dropped open.

Gus has completely changed from a sweet, cuddly rug into a snarling beast, bent on biting the man's long skateboard. His happy expression has become a mask of fury, lips stretched back, teeth bared. I'm having a hard time pulling him back because the skateboarder's insistent confrontation smells and sounds like danger to him—a primeval instinct I can't civilize despite our years of training.

I'm trying to walk on, but Gus is straining and finally achieves the extra few inches, his teeth meeting wood. He thrusts and parries a few more times before I'm able to pull him back and away. I'm dragging him now, closing my ears to the skateboarder, who's still shouting at us.

I keep walking, breathing louder than the skateboarder's shouts. My hands tremble, fingers numb from gripping the leash. He may have someone with him, also boarding, but I can't be sure. It happens so fast I can't remember exactly. Whirring skateboards anywhere around Gus's ears—surprising him—are tantamount to terror. Gus keeps turning his head back to see if the skateboard is following us. He squats for a moment on the grass to relieve himself. Steady streams of people maneuver around us and reconverge ahead.

I re-encounter the threesome, now sitting on a park bench. They smile broadly at us. We are their show...a dog gone crazy. Gus sniffs their feet. "Beautiful dog!" the tall guy says, arms draped along the back of the bench, each arm around a girl.

Advancing toward home, I try to compose myself, wracking my brain for techniques to keep this from reoccurring. Once home, I hang up Gus's leash, sigh with relief, and call a few friends to discuss the incident.

"No dog likes skateboards" is one friend's remark.

Another suggests, "From now on, walk the lake when it's not as crowded."

Another, "If that jerk wants to board on the wrong path, call the police."

I can't forget. I order a skateboard online. It arrives, green with orange wheels, disappointingly small and benign, more like a toy than the three-foot-long, sloping speed demon that terrified Gus. I think I'll have to work him into approaching the board, but he happily munches his entire dinner right off the little skateboard with no fear or aggression. I trade in an old set of Rollerblades for a longer board. I roll it a few times in front of him. No problem.

Danny and I had a lifetime of fun-loving, affectionate, loyal Beardies. As herding dogs, they all wanted order and togetherness. Splitting off in different directions in the middle of a walk is a sheepdog's signal to round us up. Several of our dogs nipped at the heels of people who appeared to be running away from them. Sylvester was terrified of groaning ice. When skateboards became popular, it presented a whole new challenge, suddenly a serious one. One of our females, Sasha, was terrified of skateboards and ran away, panicked, for hours when one whizzed past our house. A neighbor a few miles away called us when they found her.

Now, after a few days' hiatus from the lake crowd, I feel brave enough to walk Lake Calhoun again. Minneapolis is even showier, but cooler and windier, than a few days before. Eagles dive for fish; hundreds of coots are bobbing in the water, gathering to migrate. I have plenty of treats in the bag slung over my shoulder. I am prepared.

It comes to me too late—halfway around—that I should be walking against traffic to see what's coming. Instead of turning back, I press on. Gus anxiously checks over his shoulder every few feet. *I'm making Gus neurotic.*

There he is, the same skateboarder, without sunglasses, holding onto the rear rack of a girlfriend's bicycle frame, smoothly coasting on his board on the upper path, casually tapping away on his cell phone. Gus immediately yanks me toward him. He looks up, his black eyes mocking us. I squint to see him better. His beard and hair are also black, cropped short, defining a strong jaw. He is pale-skinned, wearing a stocking cap, black tee shirt, and black long pants. *Mephisto. Tormenting us, the heroic dog therapy team.* He's been looking for us. He says something to his girlfriend, who slows her bike down, keeping apace of us, trying to incite us.

In California, a student argued loudly with me in front of class about his grade. It didn't take much to flip from order to chaos during seventh period—forty-five teenagers on a Friday afternoon with weekend on their minds. He stretched his long arms across my desk, glaring at me, captive.

"I'm going to report you," he said in a deep voice, drilling holes into my gut.

"Make an appointment with me to discuss this sensibly. Sit down! Now!" I said slowly, matter-of-factly, peering around him as the rest of the class jabbered into a clamor and stuffed their books into their backpacks. Fifteen minutes before the bell. Too late to call the office. Too early to dismiss class. I stood up. He lurched toward me and growled, teeth bared. The class broke into laughter.

"Hey, you don't belong on the lake! You're a menace," the boarder yells.

What does he do to make me the loser? He's just like that kid in class. I wrap the leash around my wrist, watching my hand turn white.

He continues his bullying censure. "You have no control over your dog. Anyone with an aggressive dog has no business being on the lake. I'm on the right path now. Your dog's crazy. Look at him, lady! You can't control him! He already attacked me once!"

Rollerbladers slow their pace, applying their heel brakes, to move around him.

Gus is amped up. Too many wheels. Too much sound. I shout back, "Oh, just shut up! Mind your own business and leave me alone!" I quicken my pace, move up off the walking path, cross the upper path, and cross the street to the sidewalk. Loons fly overhead, calling to each other, lifting my heart to the sky, reminding me no creature can be or should be completely tamed.

The boarder turns his whole body around to watch me. *If I let myself go, I'll be sorry.* Epithets fill my mouth like crusts of hardtack bread. Obscenities. My breath is shallow. I hear myself panting. Adrenaline surges at high tide. Gus rears up. Ready to charge. I tighten my grip on his leash. Can't drop my shoulders. I'm ready for war. *Fight or flight.*

There's no point. He's younger. Faster. I choose flight. Speed up. He slows down. *Any moment he'll get off his board, abandon his girlfriend, run after me across the grass, carrying his board. Gus will bite his board and him. I'll be up shit creek. No witness. Just Gus.* I run-walk across the street, elude him, racing home. Again he's chased me home, afraid.

If Danny were alive, he'd have made a joke of it and quelled my fears. I'd see the whole thing as a fluke, not an ongoing threat. But I'm alone now.

For the next week, when we walk, Gus acts like a paranoid schizophrenic, jerking his head around to look behind him every twenty yards. The lake is large, 5.1 kilometers around—approximately 1100 yards rounding down. Thus, Gus is turning to look behind him at least fifty-five times.

What am I doing to my dog? The sonuvabitch skateboarder doesn't own the !@#$%^&* lake!

I stay off the lake again, watching happy joggers and dogwalkers from my window where I can view the parade. Gus and I walk in the neighborhood again, away from the lake.

I can't imagine coming home to an empty house. It was so quiet after Danny died. No oxygen tank wheezing. No phone conversations drifting from his study. No television blaring. I still listen for his heavy breathing at night. Every ambulance whining past our house reminds me of Danny's last trip to the hospital. Gus keeps me from getting stuck in the doldrums. He drags a toy or tosses a ball at me and I'm back to now.

One day we're waiting on the front steps for a friend. A small, blue truck rolls into an open spot on the curb next to my house. Cute little truck. A young man, dark-haired, no hat, closely shaven, hops out of the driver's seat, skateboard in hand. He slams it down and flies past, waving. Not thinking, I wave back. He stops and approaches. Oh no! I stand up. He's smiling.

Not the same man, I assure myself.

Approximately the same age and height as the other guy. In his twenties. Dark hair. My heart races. I didn't really see the other guy close up, just parts—his eyes, his beard, his chin. It was hard to see the whole of him. *This guy has a completely different affect.*

"If you're going to talk to me, please get off your skateboard. My dog, Gus, is very afraid of skateboards and wants to eat them on sight." He steps off his board.

"I love dogs." He holds his board behind his back. Approaches. Gus is barking.

"Thank you very much. Here, do you mind? Just hand it to me and he won't bother you." He hands off the board. It's heavier than a full grocery bag.

"I've been hoping to desensitize Gus. Even bought one, but it's a short board and the ones around the lake are long. Gus is eating his meals on a little green board with orange wheels. My training sessions are fruitless."

"I may have an old one at home you can use. Hi, Gus—how old is he?"

"Four."

"Great. I'd be happy to help you out." We exchange names and emails. He says he's a student at a local university. He offers his hand. I put the skateboard in it. He turns away and boards down the street.

My God, angels come in all forms. I study him, holding Gus back. *He's exactly what we need. How could I get so lucky?* Petals are falling in the fast wind. I remember a storm is forecast.

As he approaches the upper path, I see another boarder closing the distance between them. He's dark too. With a beard. As they continue down the path, I can swear I see the two merge into a single silhouette, but I can't really tell for sure. My eyes are old. I've seen a lot.

He knows where I live.

I lead Gus over to the little blue truck parked at the curb and tap the license plate number into "notes" on my cell phone.

At least I'll have that. At least I can give that to the police.

A View from the Porch
EARLY AUTUMN, OLD PINES

Nine p.m. It's a windless night, sawtooth aspen and white pine branches quiet. Whippoorwills hoot in the distance. Whip-whip-oor-will, whip-whip-oor-will-will-will. A variety of frogs fills in and a clatter of sandhill cranes augments this elegant lakeside orchestra.

Cranberry Lake is painted with delicate shell pink across the Western horizon where the sun went down, the color of a new kitten's paws before it has scampered across earth. A swelling moon casts its reflection across the water. No boats, no people are in sight, just the glow from a small white house alit across the shore. Everything smells fresh through the screens. My skin tingles.

I survey my husband's projects from here: a new door with a spring latch leading out to the balcony, riprap along the beach, a railing descending to the dock with little solar lights in a lovely curving line, a beautiful bench for us when we get old and need to rest on the landing. I miss him when I'm here alone, but imagine him in the yard, driving his John Deere around, smiling from ear to ear in boyish joy, or at the table saw, pencil over one ear.

At four in the morning, the loons will begin their chorus. "Hoo-woo…Hoo-woo-oo," in ascending tones—

call and response. I am soothed by their études, challenged by the puzzle of their language, head to head, love-talking. In late summer, they assemble in greater numbers to sing, planning their autumn journey.

Our 3 dogs sleep in their respective spots: huddled up in a corner of my study, ever ready by the front door, and under the dining room table. I call Dru, who has known me since I was five, to report in on the day. She's alone too, at her place on Madeline Island. "When you see the full moon, you really know you're part of the cosmos," she says. "You could go anytime and it'll still be there."

Tomorrow, I'll walk the dogs, admire ruffled hazelnuts decorating Cranberry Lane, munch an occasional blackberry, pluck a bent-over black-eyed Susan, and return, dragging fallen brush to the firepit, staining my hands and feet. My reward is a refreshing swim across the lake. After that, I'll find time to read or play the electric piano. As our former neighbor, who died last December as a centenarian, said, "It's not for everyone."

Every summer day, if there's no lightning, I swim across the lake at least once, often twice. It isn't far, it isn't smart to swim alone, and it isn't possible to save me if I were drowning. But, by the time you get a boat to me or an ambulance to our door, I'd be long gone. I can't think of a better way to slip out of sight.

Every trip brings new discoveries. Last week, our granddaughter discovered a snakeskin on the road, laid it on a rock, and exclaimed. "Look! There's the spot where his eyes were." Later, I spied busy nuthatches pecking a large hole in a tree trunk for their nest. Together, we identified a yellow wildflower called Johnny Go to Bed at Noon. And later, life jacketed and ready, she pulled and reached her arms out ahead of her until she could make it to the swimming raft. "What courage!" Dru said when I described it. "Not everyone has such courage!"

Being alone between visitors sharpens my appetite for the mystery of darkness, wondering which little rodent leaves tiny tracks along the sand and what creature splashes loudly at five a.m. Maybe a fisher. My eyes and ears are usually alert for scampering deer or black bears prowling about in the woods. After all, I am only one of many residents.

I'll never know much. I'll never stop being a little scared. I'll never stop listening and smelling and feeling the magnificence of our lake home wilderness, recognizing that it really doesn't belong to us at all. Maybe it's like Dru says—long after our porch has surrendered to the mossy, pinecone-strewn earth, we'll rise to the cosmos right up there with the moon.

Thank You

Special thanks to all of you who have listened to my stories, become subjects, encouraged me, and offered your wisdom over the years. The Altoids: Pam Backstrom, Lucy Bruntjen, Bobbie Dahl, Mary Noll, Margaret Ward, Eleanor Winston; the 42nd St. Writers' Group; Toni McNaron and the No Name Book Club; the Writers' Dinner Party: Kathy Sevig; Lucia Wilkes Smith; Susan Schierts; Grace Rogers; Dru Sweetser; Megan Thygeson; Jane Zingale. Thanks to Mildred Light Lohmann, who always believed in me.

Thank you, Stevan V. Nikolic, for knowing what really matters.

Thank you to all the animals who have shared my world, most recently, Oliver, who carries laughter in his coat and mischief in his eyes.

And to my beautiful family, this book is a tribute to your future. May you love and find beauty in the animal world and our environment, every day throughout your lives: Eddie, Stephanie, Howard, Eleanor, Eliah, Randolph, Erin, Samuel, Isaac, Joshua, Heather, and Bowie.

About the Author

Carolyn Light Bell is a writer, photographer, and educator. Her stories, set in unpredictable landscapes, portray colorful encounters that expose the sensitivities of all creatures. She has published poetry, essays and short stories in many print and online magazines. Her awards include the Croton-on-Hudson Review Award, Allen Ginsberg Award for Poetry, Editor's Choice Award for Poetry.com. Ms. Light Bell is the author of a collection of poetry DELIVERY, and two children's books: ELEANOR AND THE LITTLE TORTUGA and LALA AND HER FRIENDS.